Awful Auntie

From Yusha
To Naaya ✗

— 2022

David Walliams

Awful
Auntie

Illustrated by Tony Ross

HarperCollins *Children's Books*

First published in hardback in Great Britain in 2014
by HarperCollins *Children's Books*
HarperCollins *Children's Books* is a division of HarperCollins*Publishers* Ltd,
77-85 Fulham Palace Road, Hammersmith, London W6 8JB

Visit us on the web at
www.harpercollins.co.uk

1

ISBN 978-0-00-745361-0

Printed and bound in Australia by
Griffin Press

For Maya, Elise and Mitch

Thank yous

I would like to thank the following people.
Charlie Redmayne, the big boss at HarperCollins.
Ann-Janine Murtagh, who is the head of children's books there.
Ruth Alltimes, my brilliant editor.
The great Tony Ross, who has once again brought the story alive with the most magical illustrations.
Kate Clarke, the cover designer.
Elorine Grant, who designed the inside of the book.
Geraldine Stroud and Sam White, who are in charge of publicity.
Paul Stevens, my literary agent at Independent.
Tanya Brennand-Roper, who produces the audio versions of my books.
Finally, of course, a huge thank you to Mrs Barbara Stoat, who writes all my books for me.
I do hope you enjoy this one. I haven't read it myself so I have absolutely no clue as to what it's about.
David Walliams

This is Saxby Hall, where our story takes place.

Here is the
interior of
Saxby Hall.

This is a map of the house and grounds.

SAXBY HALL

DRIVEWAY

GARAGE

LAKE

PERIMETER WALL

Prologue

Do you have an awful auntie? One that never allows you to stay up to watch your favourite television programme? Or an aunt who makes you eat up every last spoonful of her revolting rhubarb crumble, even though she knows you hate rhubarb? Maybe your aunt gives her pet poodle a big slobbering wet kiss and then immediately gives you a big slobbering wet kiss too? Or does your aunt scoff all the most delicious chocolates from the box, leaving you with just the dreaded black cherry liqueur? Perhaps your aunt demands you wear that horrendously itchy jumper she knitted for you at Christmas? The one which reads 'I Love My Auntie' in huge purple letters on the front?

However awful your auntie might be, she will never be in the same league of awfulness as Aunt Alberta.

Aunt Alberta is the most awful aunt who ever lived.

Would you like to meet her?

Yes? I thought you would.

Here she is in all her awful awfulness...

Sharp black eyes

Monocle

Great Bavarian Mountain Owl

Deer-stalker hat

Red hair

Permanent Snarl

Pipe

Owl Pendant

Thick Leather Glove

Tweed Jacket

Plus Fours

Steel-toe-capped boots

Are you sitting uncomfortably? Then I will begin...

Meet the other characters in this story…

The young
Lady Stella Saxby.

This is Soot. He is a
chimney sweep.

Wagner is a Great Bavarian Mountain Owl.

Gibbon is the ancient butler of Saxby Hall.

Detective Strauss is a policeman.

I

Frozen

It was all a blur.

At first there were only colours.

Then lines.

Slowly through the haze of Stella's gaze the room eventually took shape.

The little girl realised she was lying in her own bed. Her bedroom was just one of countless in this vast country house. To her right side stood her wardrobe, on her left sat a tiny dressing table, framed by a tall window. Stella knew her bedroom as well as she knew her

own face. Saxby Hall had always been her home. But somehow, at this moment, everything seemed strange.

Outside there was not a sound. The house had never been this quiet before. All was silent. From her bed Stella turned her head to look out of the window.

All was white. Thick snow had fallen. It had covered everything within sight – the long sloping lawn, the huge deep lake, and the empty fields beyond the estate.

Icicles hung from the branches of trees. Everything was frozen.

The sun was nowhere to be seen. The sky was as pale as clay. It seemed to be not quite night, not quite day. Was it early morning or late evening? The little girl had no idea.

Stella felt as if she had been asleep forever. Was it days? Months? Years? Her mouth was as dry as a desert. Her body felt as heavy as stone. As still as a statue.

For a moment the little girl thought she might still be asleep and dreaming. Dreaming she was awake in her bedroom. Stella had experienced that dream before, and it was frightening because try as she might she couldn't move. Was this the same nightmare again? Or something more sinister?

To test whether she was asleep and dreaming, the girl thought she would try to move. Starting at the far end of her body, first she tried to waggle her little toe. If she was awake and she thought about waggling her toe it would just waggle. But try as she might it wouldn't waggle, or wiggle. Or even woggle. One by one she tried to move each toe on her left foot, and then each toe on her right. One by one they all point-blank refused to do anything. Feeling increasingly panicked she tried to circle her ankles, before attempting to stretch her legs, then to bend her knees and finally

she concentrated as hard as she could on lifting her arms. All were impossible. It was as if she had been buried in sand from the neck down.

Beyond her bedroom door, Stella heard a sound. The house dated back centuries, it had been passed through many generations of the Saxby family. It was so old that everything creaked, and so vast that every noise echoed down the endless labyrinth of corridors. Sometimes the young Stella believed that the house was haunted. That a ghost stalked Saxby Hall in the dead of night. When she went to bed, the little girl was convinced she could hear someone or something moving about behind her wall. Sometimes she would even hear a voice, calling to her. Terrified, she would dash into her mother and father's room, and climb into bed with them. Her mother and father would hold Stella tight, and tell her she was not to worry her pretty little head. All those strange noises were just the clatter of pipes and the creaking of floorboards.

Stella was not so sure.

Her eyes darted over to the huge oak-panelled door of her bedroom. At waist height there was a keyhole, though she never locked the door and didn't even know where the key was. Most likely it had been lost a hundred years ago by some great-great-great-grandparent. One of those Saxby lords or ladies whose paintings were hung every few paces along the corridors, captured forever unsmiling in oils.

The keyhole flickered light to dark. The little girl thought she saw the white of an eyeball staring at her through the hole before quickly disappearing out of view.

"Mama? Is that you?" she cried out. Hearing her own voice out loud, Stella knew this was no dream.

On the other side of the door an eerie silence lingered.

Stella plucked up the courage to speak again. "Who is it?" she pleaded. "Please?" The floorboards creaked outside. Someone or something had been spying on her through the keyhole.

The handle turned, and slowly the door was pushed open. The bedroom was dark, but the hallway was light, so at first all the girl could see was a silhouette.

It was the outline of someone as wide as they were tall. Even though they were extremely wide they still weren't particularly tall. The figure was wearing a tailored jacket and plus fours (those long billowy shorts that golfers sometimes wear). A deer-stalker hat adorned the figure's head, with the ear flaps unflatteringly down. Jutting out from their mouth was a long thick pipe. Soon plumes of sickly sweet tobacco smoke clouded the room. On one hand there was a thick leather glove. Perched on the glove was the unmistakeable outline of an owl.

Stella knew instantly who this person was. It was her awful aunt, Alberta.

"Well, you have finally woken up, child," said Aunt Alberta. The woman's voice was rich and deep, like a boozy cake. She stepped out of the doorway and into her niece's bedroom, her large brown steel-toe-capped boots clumping on the floorboards.

Now in the half-light Stella could make out the heavy tweed of her suit, and the long sharp talons of

the owl wrapped around the fingers of the glove. It was a Great Bavarian Mountain Owl, the largest species of owl there was. In the villages of Bavaria these owls were known by locals as 'flying bears' on account of their startling size. The owl's name was Wagner. It was an unusual name for an unusual pet, but then Aunt Alberta was a highly unusual person.

"How long have I been asleep please, Auntie?" asked Stella.

Aunt Alberta took a long suck on her pipe, and smiled. "Oh, just a few months, child."

II

A Baby Vanishes

Before we continue our story, I need to tell you a little more about Aunt Alberta, and why she was so awful.

This is the Saxby family tree.

LORD CUTHBERT SAXBY
(1698–1755)

LADY JANE SAXBY
(NÉE WHITTINGDON)

LADY ROSAMUND SAXBY
(NÉE MOORE)

LORD HORTATIO SAXBY
(1742–1815)

HUMPHREY
(1742–1850)

HORACE
(1743–1801)

HONORA
(1748–1823)

LORD CEDRIC SAXBY
(1799–1862)

LADY GENEVIEVE SAXBY
(NÉE CRUTTINGDOWN-
SMYTHE)

LADY HENRIETTA SAXBY
(NÉE GORRINGTON)

LORD OSCAR SAXBY
(1842–1925)

OSBERT
(1844–1914)

OCTAVIA
(1845–1846)

ALBERTA
(1868–)

HERBERT
(1880–?)

LORD CHESTER SAXBY
(1880–)

LADY EMILY SAXBY
(NÉE SMYTHE)

SAXBY
FAMILY TREE

STELLA
(1920–)

As you can see from the family tree, Alberta was the eldest of three children. She was the first-born child of Lord and Lady Saxby, followed by her twin brothers Herbert and Chester. A dreadful fate befell Herbert – the first-born twin – as a baby. As the oldest male child, Herbert was destined to take the title of Lord Saxby when his father eventually passed away. With the title came riches too – the family home, Saxby Hall, and all the jewels and silver that had been passed down the generations. The laws of inheritance ruled that the first-born boy of the family was given everything.

However, soon after Herbert was born the most mysterious thing happened. The baby vanished in the dead of night. His doting mother had put him to bed in his cot, but when she came into his nursery in the morning he had simply disappeared. Wracked with pain she screamed the house down.

"Aaaaaaaaaaarrrrrrr rrrrgggggggggghhhhhhh hhhhhhhhhhhhhhh!!!!!!"

Folk from the neighbouring towns and villages streamed out of their houses to help the search. They combed the surrounding countryside for the infant day and night for weeks, but no trace of him was ever found.

Alberta was twelve when her baby brother disappeared. Nothing in the house was ever the same again. It was not just that little Herbert was gone, it was the not knowing what had happened to him that hurt his parents the most. Of course they still had Chester (Stella's father), but the pain of losing their beautiful baby boy never left them.

The case became one of the great unsolved mysteries of the age.

Wild theories swirled around the baby's disappearance. The young Alberta swore she had heard howling outside on the lawn that night. The girl was convinced a wolf had taken her baby brother in the dead of night. However, no wolves were found within a hundred miles of Saxby Hall. Soon this theory became just one of many. Some supposed that a visiting circus troupe had kidnapped Herbert, and disguised him as a clown. Others believed that the infant had somehow climbed out of his cot and crawled out of the house. Most unlikely of all was the suspicion some had that the boy had been spirited away by a gang of evil elves.

None of this wild speculation helped bring Herbert home. Years passed. Life went on, though not for Herbert's mother and father. The night of the disappearance froze the lord and lady in time. They were never seen in public again. Putting on their happy faces became impossible. The sense of loss, the not knowing; it was unbearable. The lord and lady could

barely sleep or eat. They roamed around Saxby Hall like ghosts. In the end they were said to have died of broken hearts.

III

A Beastly Child

With baby Herbert gone, Chester (Stella's father) became the heir. Growing up, Alberta was absolutely beastly to him. As a child she would:

– Give her little brother a highly poisonous tarantula spider for Christmas.

– Collect rocks and dust them
with icing sugar. Then give
one to her younger brother
to eat pretending it was a
rock cake.

– Peg him to the washing line
and let him dangle there
all afternoon.

– Chop down a tree
while he was climbing it.

– Play hide-and-seek with him. Alberta would let the boy hide and then she would go on holiday.

– Shove him in the lake when his back was turned feeding the ducks.

– Replace the candles on his birthday cake with sticks of dynamite.

– Swing him around the playroom
by his ankles as fast
as she could and then
let go.

– Cut the brake
cables on his
bicycle.

– Force-feed him a
bowl of live worms
saying it was
'special spaghetti'.

– During a snowball fight,
cover cricket balls
in ice then
hurl them
at him.

– Lock him in a wardrobe,
and then push it down
a flight of stairs.

 – Put earwigs in his ears while
he was sleeping so he would
wake up screaming.

– Bury him up to his neck in sand at the beach, then
leave him there as the tide came in.

Despite all this Chester was always kind to his sister. When Lord and Lady Saxby died and he eventually inherited Saxby Hall from his parents, he was determined to look after the old place as best he could. The new Lord Saxby loved the house as much as his parents always had. But because Chester was by nature such a generous man he gave the family's huge treasure trove of silver and jewels to his sister Alberta.

Altogether it was worth thousands and thousands of pounds. However, within a short while, the woman had lost it all.

That's because Alberta had a dangerous obsession.

Tiddlywinks.

It was a very popular game at the time. Tiddlywinks was played with a pot and different sized discs or 'winks'.

The aim was to use your large wink, named a 'squidger', to propel as many of the smaller winks into the pot as you could. From childhood, Alberta would force Chester to play with her. To stop her hurling the pot of winks across the room if she lost, Chester would always let her win. Alberta was not only a very bad loser, she was also a cheat. As a child she created

her own tiddlywinks moves, all of them completely
against the rules:

'Whipple-scrump' –
to eat your opponent's
squidger.

'Gnash-gnosh' –
to bite your opponent's
hand while they try to play.

'Knicker-knocker-glory' –
hiding all your opponent's
winks in your knickers.

'Boom-shack-a-lack' – to fire your winks into the pot
with an air rifle.

'Winkferno' – to burn
all your opponent's
winks.

'Knee-thumper' – to
make the tiddlywinks
table shake when it's
your opponent's turn by
bashing it with your knee.

'Snatcheroo' – when your opponent's wink is in mid
flight and a highly trained bird of prey catches it in
its bill.

'Sticky-wink' – gluing your opponent's winks to the table.

'Gigantopot' – when your opponent is not looking, replace the pot with one that is much taller making it impossible for them to fire any winks in.

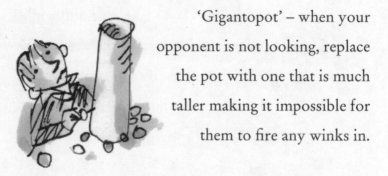

'Poot' – to break wind on your opponent's squidger, thus rendering it unusable for a short while.

One Christmas, Chester bought his big sister *The Tiddlywinks Rulebook* by Professor T. Wink. His hope was that together they could consult the rules, and her terrible cheating would cease. However, Alberta point-blank refused to even open the book. *The Tiddlywinks Rulebook* gathered dust on a shelf of the huge library of Saxby Hall.

Ever since she was a child, Alberta was ridiculously competitive. She had to win. Again and again and again.

"I am the best. **B, E, E, S, T!**" she would chant. Her spelling was always atrocious. However, this aggressive desire to conquer everyone else is what ended up costing her relatives dear. As soon as she got her hands on some of the Saxby family fortune, thanks to Chester's kindness, she gambled it away. Alberta played at the high-stakes tiddlywinks tables at the casinos of Monte Carlo. Within a week the woman had lost everything she had. Thousands upon thousands of pounds. Next she sneaked into her brother's study and pinched his chequebook. Forging his signature, Alberta secretly stole all the money out of Chester's bank account. Within days she had lost her brother's money too. Every last penny. The family was plunged into terrible debt, from which it was impossible to recover.

As a result, Chester was forced to sell all the possessions he possibly could. Antiques, paintings, fur coats, even his beloved wife's diamond engagement

ring, all went to auction houses so Lord Saxby could fight to keep the family home. A home that had been in the Saxby family for centuries. Like any great house, Saxby Hall employed an army of staff to keep it running – a cook, a gardener, a nanny, a chauffeur and a platoon of maids. However, with all the money squandered by Alberta, they simply couldn't be paid any more. The bank demanded they all be fired immediately. So with a heavy heart Chester had to let them go.

Except one. The ancient butler, Gibbon.

Lord Saxby tried to give Gibbon his notice a dozen times or more. However, the servant was so old, just short of a hundred, that he had become very deaf and blind. As a result it was impossible to tell him to go. Even if you shouted right into his ear, the poor old soul wouldn't hear a thing. Gibbon had worked for the Saxbys for generations. He had been in service for them for so long, he had become part of the family. Chester had grown up with Gibbon looking after him, and loved him dearly, like he was an eccentric old uncle. Secretly he was overjoyed that Gibbon stayed at the house, not least because he was sure the ancient butler had nowhere else to go.

So Gibbon continued to roam Saxby Hall carrying on with his duties, though in a totally topsy-turvy way. Gibbon would:

– Mow the carpet
with a lawnmower.

– Bring in a tray piled
high with dirty socks
and announce,
"Afternoon tea, m'lord."

– Iron the plants.

– Water the sofa.

– Bang a gong
in the middle
of the night
to announce,
"Dinner is served."

– Serve a boiled
billiards ball
in an egg cup
at breakfast.

– Polish the grass.

– Boil your shoes.

– Pick up the lampshade and say "Saxby Ball, who is speaking please?" as if it was a telephone.

– Take the rug for a walk.

– Put the chicken to roast in the boot of the Rolls Royce.

Stella's mother and father worked tirelessly, day and night, to care for the house and grounds, but Saxby Hall was just too big for them. Inevitably it fell into disrepair. Soon they had a huge house they couldn't afford to heat or light, and an old Rolls Royce they could barely afford to run. Through his considerable charm Chester, now Lord Saxby, just managed to keep the angry bank manager in London at bay.

When Stella was born he was determined that his daughter would one day inherit this great house, as he had from his father. Of course his sister Alberta had shown she couldn't be trusted with Saxby Hall, so Chester made sure his wishes were crystal clear in his will.

The Will of Lord Saxby of Saxby Hall.

I, Lord Chester Mandrake Saxby, do hereby leave the family home, Saxby Hall, to my daughter Stella Amber Saxby. In the event of Stella's untimely passing, the house should be sold and all the money given to the poor. It is my express wish that my sister, Alberta Hettie Dorothea Pansy Colin Saxby, should not inherit the house, as she will only gamble it away playing tiddlywinks. To ensure this does not happen, the deeds of ownership to Saxby Hall have been concealed in the house, somewhere my sister Alberta will never ever find them.

Signed the day of Monday 1st of January 1921

Lord Chester Mandrake Saxby

Lord Saxby kept this will top secret from his sister. If she ever read it, it would be sure to plunge her into a terrible rage.

IV

The Great Bavarian Mountain Owl

Now how did Aunt Alberta come to have a Great Bavarian Mountain Owl as a pet, I hear you ask. To answer that, I'll need to take you back in time once more, to before young Stella was born.

Soon after Alberta had lost all the family's money at the tiddlywinks tables of Monte Carlo, Europe was thrust into war. Chester joined the army as an officer, and was awarded a chestful of medals for his bravery on the battlefields of France. Meanwhile his sister also enlisted, and found herself fighting in the forests of Bavaria as a machine-gunner. Unusually for someone who was British, she chose to fight on the German side. Alberta's only reason was that she 'preferred

the German uniforms'.
She felt she looked
smokin' hot in one of
the German army's
spiked helmets, called
Pickelhauben. You can
judge for yourselves…

One thing she had often done as a child was to
steal rare birds' eggs. Alberta knew that the Great
Bavarian Mountain Owl was one of the rarest birds in
the world. So when she spotted one
nesting in the forest where she was
posted she climbed the tree and
stole the egg out of its nest.
Then she sat on it until it
hatched, and named the
little owlet 'Wagner', after
her favourite German
composer.*

The composer's name was 'Wagner'. Keep up.

The war ended soon after. Alberta had been fighting for the losing side, and the prospect of being sent to a prisoner-of-war camp did not appeal. So she stole a Zeppelin, one of the huge German military airships. With the little owlet Wagner safely under her arm, she took to the air. At first all went well, she piloted the Zeppelin hundreds of miles over mainland Europe. However, while flying over the English Channel with the white cliffs of Dover in sight, disaster struck. The metal spike on her helmet burst the huge gas cell above her. Instantly the

Zeppelin started violently spurting hot air. The airship was really nothing more than a giant balloon after all. It farted its way across the sky at terrific speed, before crash-landing into the

sea with a
PLOP.

Alberta just managed to swim to shore, the owlet (still larger than the average owl) perched precariously on her head.

Once safely back at Saxby Hall she began training the bird. Wagner never knew his real owl parents, but quickly accepted Alberta as his mother. Indeed the woman would feed the owlet live worms and spiders from her mouth, passing them from lip to bill. As Wagner grew, so did the treats. Soon she would feed him mice and sparrows she had caught in traps. Food became a reward, and over time Alberta had taught her owl a number of impressive tricks:

– Fetching her slippers.

– Flying a loop-the-loop.

– Aerial reconnaissance (a military term she had picked up when fighting in World War One, which meant spying from the air).

– Dive-bombing children's kites.

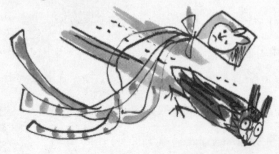

– Stealing old ladies'

knickers from washing lines.

– Dropping stink-bombs

from the air at the village's

summer fete.

– Delivering a letter
or parcel within a
hundred-mile radius.

– Duetting with her on her favourite
German opera arias. This was
painful to listen to as Aunt Alberta
was an even worse singer than the owl.

– To use a special owl urinal when having
an owl pee.

– To swoop on kittens
and devour them in
one gulp, bones and all.

– To make an
apple strudel.

THE GREAT BAVARIAN MOUNTAIN OWL

YELLOW EYES

MASSIVE EAR TUFTS

LARGE HEAD

BROWN AND GREY FEATHERS

RAZOR SHARP BEAK

MASSIVE BREAST

POINTY TALONS

WEIGHT OF 6½ STONE

HEIGHT OF APPROX. 4 FT

'Owling', 'Owlery', 'Owlcraft', 'Owlistry', 'Owlography', 'Owlosophy', call it what you will, Alberta became an expert.*

---

*Or 'Owlpert' to use the correct terminology (or 'Owlology').

Soon she and her beloved Wagner became famous in owling circles. They even started doing photoshoots for specialist bird of prey publications, such as *My Owl, Just Owls, Owl!, Owls Owls Owls, Owls Only, Mature Owls,* and *Owling Monthly: The Magazine for Owls and their Admirers.* Once they even appeared together on the cover of *Twit-Woo!,* very much the

Hello! magazine of the owl world. Inside there were twelve pages of 'at home with' photographs, and a lengthy interview where they talked about how they had met and their hopes for their future together. Of course Wagner's answers were all in squawks.

Alberta and Wagner. Wagner and Alberta. It was a very close relationship.

The pair travelled everywhere together on Alberta's

motorcycle, with Wagner in the sidecar. Both had matching leather flying helmets and goggles.

What was more unusual still was that Alberta and Wagner also shared a bed. When Stella would bring her aunt her nightly glass of sherry, Alberta and Wagner would be tucked up together in matching striped pyjamas reading the day's newspapers. It was a bizarre sight. Another time Stella heard the two of them splashing around in the bath together. It wasn't natural, it wasn't right, and it definitely couldn't be hygienic. Especially not for the owl.

However, this closeness between man and beast was not without purpose. For all this time, Aunt Alberta was training her owl to obey her every command. Even to do unspeakable evil.

V

Mummified

Now we have learned all about Alberta and her Great Bavarian Mountain Owl, we can return to our story.

Up in Stella's bedroom, at the top of Saxby Hall, the little girl was laid out on her bed. A deep shadow loomed over her. The shadow of her Aunt Alberta, with her pet owl Wagner perched on her hand.

Stella's voice cracked as she asked her aunt, "I don't understand. How can I have been asleep for months?"

Alberta thought for a moment, and took a live mouse out of her pocket by its tail before dropping it into Wagner's mouth. The bird wolfed the unfortunate creature whole.

"Ever since the accident…" replied the woman.

"Accident?! What accident?" Stella pleaded.

Aunt Alberta approached the girl's bed, and rested a hand on the blanket.

"The accident that did this to you…"

With a theatrical flourish the woman whipped the blanket off the bed. Stella looked down in horror to see that her entire body was bandaged up. It was as if she was an ancient Egyptian pharaoh, mummified in a pyramid.

"Every bone in your body has been broken."

"Nooooo…!" cried the girl.

"Yeeeesssss…!" replied Alberta, mocking her niece's tone. "Each little bone was shattered into hundreds of pieces. You had to be scooped up like a piece of wibbly-wobbly jelly!"

"How on…? W-w-what happened? And where are Mama and Papa?" pleaded Stella. The little girl had so many questions her words were tumbling out in desperation.

Aunt Alberta merely smirked. She sucked on her pipe and blew some smoke into her niece's face. "Oh! So many questions! All in good time, child."

"But I need to know!" demanded Stella. "Now!"

Alberta tutted. "Perhaps you would like a game of tiddlywinks first!"

The girl couldn't believe what she was hearing. "What are you talking about?"

The woman pulled a box off the girl's shelf and put it down on the bed.

"This isn't the time!" said Stella.

"There's always time for tiddlywinks!" replied Alberta, as she busied herself arranging all the pieces of the game. "My go first!" she said excitedly, as she pushed down on her squidger to flip one of her winks into flight. It landed with a ping in the pot.

PING!

"A million and seven points to me. Your go!"

Stella stared at her aunt, her eyes bulging with fury.

"Oh no, silly me, I've forgotten. Both your arms are broken! Looks like I've won again."

"I never wanted to play."

"No one likes a bad loser, Stella."

"I need to know what has happened to my parents!" shouted the girl.

Alberta shook her head at her niece's behaviour. "Now if you can be quiet for just a moment, your aunty-waunty will tell you exactly what happened!" She often spoke in this baby talk. It made Stella's skin crawl. "You have no memory at all of the accident?"

"N-n-no." Try as she might Stella could not remember anything. She must have hit her head hard. But how? "Please! Tell me!"

"Oh dear. Oh dear, oh dear. Oh deary deary me."

"What?! Tell me! I'm begging you!"

"Hush! This instant!" hissed the woman.

The girl had no option but to fall silent.

"Now Auntie can begin." It was as if she was telling a bedtime story. "It was a rainy morning. You were sat in the back seat of your father's Rolls Royce, on your way into London. Your father had another appointment with the bank manager, while your mother was going to take you to see Buckingham Palace. But alas! Your jolly jaunt was not to be."

"Why? What happened?"

"Perhaps your father had been drinking…"

"He never drank!" protested Stella.

"…and he must have been driving too fast…"

"He never drove too fast!"

But Alberta was in full flow now and there was absolutely no stopping her. "The Rolls Royce was speeding along a coastal road. Your father lost control of the car on a sharp bend and…" Suddenly the woman paused, for dramatic effect. It was as if she was enjoying being the bearer of bad news.

"What?!"

"It plunged over the side of a cliff!"

"NO!" Stella screamed.

"Yes! Smashing on to the rocks below," Alberta said, before adding her own sound effect.

"BOOM!"

Stella was sobbing now.

"There there!" said Alberta, patting her niece on her head as if she were a dog. "You, child, are very lucky to be alive. Very lucky. You have been in a coma for months."

"What about Mama and Papa?" she pleaded. Stella feared the worst, but she hadn't quite given up hope yet. "Where are they? Are they here in the house? Are they in hospital?"

Alberta fixed her niece with a stare. A pained expression crossed her face.

"Oh poor, poor child." Aunt Alberta shook her head and perched on the side of the bed, her hefty frame causing the mattress to tip violently to the side. Her stubby fingers tiptoed over to her niece, and she rested her clammy palm on top of the girl's tightly bandaged hand. Tears welled in Stella's eyes. Soon those tears were streaming down her cheeks.

"Please! Tell me what's happened to my mama and papa!"

A trace of a smile crossed her aunt's face. "Now, I have some rather upsetting news about your parents…"

VI

Some Terrible Nightmare

"Dead?" Stella was in floods of tears now. "Please, please, tell me this isn't true? Tell me this is all just some terrible nightmare!"

Aunt Alberta looked upon her niece with pity. She took a long, deep puff on her pipe, as she pondered her reply. "Dead, child. As dead as dead can be. Deader than dead. Completely deadest. In fact so totally dead they were buried under the ground months ago. I don't think there is much hope for them now."

Memories of her beloved mother and father flashed through Stella's mind. Her papa taking her in a rowing boat on the lake, making her giggle as he

clowned around with the oars. Her mama twirling her around the ballroom of Saxby Hall, teaching her to dance. The memories already seemed like scratchy old black-and-white films, the pictures fuzzy and jumpy, the sound muffled. She fought to make them clearer. This was all she had left of them now.

"Months ago?" spluttered Stella. "So I missed their funeral?"

"Mmm, child. It was a terribly sad day, seeing their two cheap coffins lying side by side. Luckily the vicar gave me a discount for the funeral service as it was two people being buried in one go."

"Did you arrange some flowers from me?"

"No. To be honest with you, they were so dead by that point that they wouldn't have known."

The little girl couldn't believe what she was hearing. How could her aunt be so uncaring about her brother and his wife – Stella's dear mother and father. It was no secret she deeply resented Lord and Lady Saxby, even though they had treated her with nothing but kindness. Alberta even had a wing of Saxby Hall all to herself. Without Chester the woman would have been homeless, having squandered all her own money and plenty of her brother's. However, she never once said thank you or did anything kind in return.

Even when she was very little Stella had noticed the cruel way her aunt behaved around Chester. Alberta would roll her eyes whenever he spoke, and sneer whenever he offered her a smile. If it was someone in the family's birthday, Alberta would slink off to her very own greenhouse, at the bottom of the long sloping lawn. Unusually the woman had blacked out its windows with paint. Stella was sure this rather defeated the idea of it being a greenhouse as no sunlight could shine in. Who had ever heard of plants that could grow in the dark? Still, whatever it was that Alberta had hidden inside, it was free from everyone else's prying eyes.

"So I have been in a coma all this time?" asked Stella, her sobs slowing down a little now.

"Yes. Months now. You hit your head in the car crashy-washy, and were rushed to hospital in an ambulance. The doctors and nurses did their best for you. Of course I was on the phone to them every hour, asking for any news of my only niece, I was so worried your condition might worsen."

"But if all my bones are broken why aren't I still there?" demanded the girl.

The woman took another puff on her pipe, giving her time to think. "Because my little niecy-wiecy, who better to look after you than me? Hospitals are full of ghastly people who are all illy-willy. How much better to be at home in your own bed, under the watchful eyes of Wagner and I. Isn't that right, Wagner?"

The woman kissed her owl's bill, as she often did. Stella always found this distinctly uncomfortable to watch, and shuddered. As much as someone who was bound neck to toe in bandages could shudder.

"Wagner has looked after you so well these past few months. It was like you were his little owlet, ha ha!"

"What do you mean?" asked Stella.

"Well, being in a coma, it was hard to feed you. And I needed to, I mean *wanted* to keep you alive. So I would pop a nice juicy slug or beetle into Wagner's mouth, he would give it a good munch, and then spit it into your mouth as you slept."

The girl's face went green. "That's disgusting!"

"See the thanks we get, Wagner?" said Aunt Alberta. "Spoilt little brat. Well, we will leave you for now." With that Alberta stood up, and the bed righted itself.

"Where are you going?" demanded Stella.

"Oh, I have been rushed off my feet since your mother and father's tragic passing! It's been go-go-go! So much to do! Selling your mother's clothes, burning your father's letters and diaries."

"But I would have wanted to keep them!"

"You should have said!"

"I was in a coma!" protested Stella.

"That's no excuse. Oh and there's something I need to ask you."

"What?"

Suddenly Aunt Alberta seemed a little coy. She spoke as if choosing her words very carefully. "Well, child, I've been searching and searching for the deeds to Saxby Hall."

"Why?"

"Because this old wreck would be far too much for a young girl like you to look after. How old are you?"

"Nearly thirteen!" replied Stella.

"So, you are twelve?"

"Yes," the girl conceded.

"Well, say twelve then. A mere child. Wouldn't it be best for your favourite aunty-waunty to look after Saxby Hall for you?"

The little girl fell silent. Her father had always

told her that she would one day inherit Saxby Hall, and Stella had promised to look after it for the next generation of Saxbys. Of course she couldn't look after the house all on her own, but she didn't want Alberta to do it for her. Stella didn't trust this woman one bit.

"**But…!**" she protested.

"**No buts!** Please don't worry your pretty little head with all this. It's boring grown-ups' business! Just as soon as I've turned this whole house upside down and found the deeds to Saxby Hall, all you have to do is sign them over to me and this place is mine. I mean mine to look after for you. So my little question is this…"

"Go on."

The woman fixed a grin on her face, and it looked like she was wearing a mask. "Well, I was wondering if you knew where those little deedsy-weedsies might be?"

Stella hesitated for a moment. Her mother and father had always taught her never to tell lies. However, something deep inside her told her that right now she had to. "**No.**"

The little girl's voice went up a notch. Aunt Alberta was not convinced.

"Are you sure?" The woman brought her face right up close to her niece's. So close that Stella had to try not to breathe, such were the fumes of sherry and pipe tobacco on her aunt's breath.

"Yes," replied the girl. Stella tried her best not to blink, in case that gave her away. However, she was so unused to lying that her mouth went as dry as hot sand, and she just had to swallow.

GULP.

"If I find out that you're lying, young lady, there will be trouble. Mark my words there will be trouble. **T, R, U, B, L, E.** Trouble." Yes, spelling was certainly not Aunt Alberta's strong point.

"Now if you need anything, my dear, anything at all, just ring this bell."

Out of the patch pocket of her tweed jacket,

Alberta produced a tiny gold bell. It was in the shape of a miniature statuette of an owl. The woman teased the top, and the quietest DING-A-LING sounded.

"Either myself or Wagner will come as soon as we possibly can."

"I'm not eating any more mushed-up creepy-crawlies from that horrible bird!" shouted Stella.

The noise startled Wagner, who flapped his wings as he jumped up and down on his mistress's hand, squawking. The huge creature's wings were so long that as he flapped and squawked a picture hanging on the wall was sent flying. It fell to the floor, the glass smashing. It was a wedding photograph of Stella's mother and father. It was her absolute favourite photograph of them. They were stood outside the local church, the same one they were now buried at. In the picture they looked so young and in love, her mother achingly beautiful in her flowing white wedding dress, her father boyishly handsome in his

shiny black silk top hat and morning suit.

Aunt Alberta leaned down to pick up the photograph. "Tut-tut-tut…" she said in a pantomime of caring. "Look what you've done now, you selfish child! Startling poor little Wagner like that." The woman pulled the photograph out of the frame, and with one hand screwed it up into a ball. "I'll put this on the bonfire for you!"

"No!" screamed Stella. "Please don't!"

"It's no trouble," replied her aunt. "Now as I said before your outburst, if there's anything you need, anything at all, just ring the belly-welly."

"But how can I ring it? I can't move either of my arms!" Stella protested.

The woman leaned over the girl's bed.

"Open wide!" she ordered, as if she was a demonic dentist. Unthinking the girl did as she was told, and Aunt Alberta placed the bell into her niece's mouth.

The woman chuckled at the strange sight, and her owl squawked brightly, as if he was laughing too. The gruesome twosome giggled their way over to Stella's bedroom door, and slammed it behind them.

BANG!

Stella heard the key in the lock turn.

CLICK.

There was no escape.

VII

The Human Caterpillar

But Stella had to try to flee. Even though this great country house was her home, she didn't want to be alone here with this creepy lady a moment longer. The girl had always found Aunt Alberta spooky when growing up. The woman would sometimes tell her niece traditional bedtime stories, but with a twist. The twist was that in Alberta's versions evil would always triumph.

Hansel and Gretel
It's not the witch that is shoved in the oven at the end, but the two children. The witch lives happily ever after in her house made of sweets.

Three Little Pigs

The big bad wolf huffs and
puffs and blows all three
little piggies' houses down.
He then has roast pork
for breakfast, lunch and
dinner every day for a week.

Goldilocks and the Three Bears

When Goldilocks gobbles
up their porridge, the
bears get their revenge
by gobbling up her.

Snow White

When Snow White finds the seven dwarfs' cottage they lock her up and make her do all their cooking and cleaning. Snow White then spends the rest of her life hand-washing seven pairs of dirty dwarf underpants every day.

Sleeping Beauty

She never wakes up. Just blows off violently in her sleep. Alberta particularly enjoyed adding the sound effects on this one, even providing some with a trumpet.

Jack and the Beanstalk
Jack loses his grip on
the beanstalk while
climbing up it and
falls down to earth,
landing on top of his
mother with a giant
SPLAT!

Rapunzel
She's completely bald.
When the handsome
prince tries to climb up
the tower all he does
is pull her wig clean off.

The Frog Prince
The princess kisses the frog and
contracts a waterborne disease
that makes her bottom explode.

The Three Billy Goats Gruff
The troll who lives under the
bridge eats all the goats, then eats
the bridge, and then does a gigantic
BURP. Again Aunt Alberta always adored providing
the sound effects here.

The Little Mermaid
She drowns. The end.

These twists spoke of how Alberta herself was twisted.
Stella had to escape.

The girl waited for the sound of her aunt's footsteps to grow fainter as she disappeared down the long corridor. The bell the woman had put in her mouth had a bitter rusty taste, and she pushed it away with her tongue. It rolled down her body and rested on the top of her stomach. Stella looked down at herself. Everything below her neck was tightly wrapped in what must be miles and miles of bandage. Aunt Alberta had told her that every bone in her body was broken. But could that really be true? More likely the bandages were just a way of keeping her captive. The girl lifted her head. She could circle her neck around perfectly. Something told her that if she could only wrestle her way out of these bandages, she could make a run for it.

Saxby Hall was a few miles from the nearest village, situated beyond a huge expanse of moorland. It was too treacherous to cross at night, but during the day she might make it to the nearest farmhouse in a couple of hours if she ran as fast as she could. Stella could knock on the first door, and beg for help. The girl desperately needed to discover for herself the truth about how her parents had died.

But before she could escape from the house, Stella had to escape from the bandages.

The girl began trying to rock her body from side to side. A flicker of a smile crossed her face as she realised she could move a tiny bit.

To the left.

To the right.

To the left.

To the right.

Like a swing, she went a little further each time.

To the left.

To the right.

The bell rolled over her stomach and dropped on to the wooden floorboards below.

THUD.
DiNG!

It was a long way down to fall. Still the girl kept rolling from side to side.

To the left.   To the right.

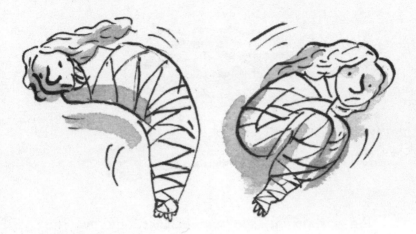

Momentum was building now.

To the left.   To the right.

To the left.

For a moment, she was balanced on her side.
Suddenly she felt weightless. Then even more suddenly
she was lying face down on the floor. THUD.

"Owww!" she cried, before cursing
herself for making a sound.

The bandages had loosened a little now, and Stella
found she could move her legs and arms a tiny bit.

That means they can't be broken! she realised. She shuffled along the floor with all the speed and grace of a caterpillar. After a minute the girl realised she had

only moved a few inches. It was pitiful. She lay on the floor, utterly exhausted and dejected. At this rate it would take a month to make it to her bedroom door, and a year to drag herself all the way downstairs.

Stella knew she wasn't going to get anywhere until she had wriggled out of these bandages. But how? She couldn't move her hands or feet. Then she had an idea.

She was going to have to bite her way out.

Stella tucked her chin down as far as it could possibly go. Next she stuck her tongue out, and tried to hook a piece of the bandage with the tip. Like trying to hook a rubber duck with a rod at the fair, it was much more difficult than it looked. After trying and trying and trying, finally she managed to catch the end of the bandage between her teeth.

Yanking her neck back she tugged at it. Shaking her head from side to side she loosened it. When she had pulled a long enough strip of bandage loose, she held it tight in her mouth. It was like she was a dog who had found a very special stick and was never letting it go.

Stella shuffled back towards her bed. Exhausted but determined, she hooked the loose piece of bandage on one of the sharp metal springs under the mattress. Next she rolled herself over. And over. The more she

rolled the more the bandage unravelled.

It was working!

With each roll she could feel her body moving that little bit more. Soon she could waggle her arms a little, then her legs.

The human caterpillar was hatching into a butterfly.

The excitement at slowly becoming free filled her tired body with an electric energy. Soon she was rolling faster and faster, and waggling her arms and legs frantically. As soon as her left arm was free she grabbed the end of the bandage with her hand.

It was unravelling at speed now.

Next her right arm came free. Now she could push

the bandage down and soon she kicked her legs free.

For a moment she lay on her back on the floor of her bedroom. The epic struggle was over. The bandage was curled up next to her, like a snake she had killed with her bare hands.

Stella's bedroom was two floors up. In her nightdress she crawled over to the window. Looking down to the snow-covered lawn she realised she was far too high up to jump.

A huge white figure loomed at the end of the long sloping garden. It looked like a snowman, but it was nearly as tall as the house. A ladder leaned next to it. What was it? Stella was transfixed by it for a moment, but darkness was descending. And there was no time to lose.

But there was a problem.

The only way out of her bedroom was the door, and it was locked.

There was only one key.

On the other side of the door.

VIII

The Great Escape

Stella had a plan. Racing over to her desk, she grabbed a pencil and a piece of paper. There was a small gap at the bottom of the heavy wooden door. Stella slipped the piece of paper through it. Then, using the sharp end of her pencil, she gently poked the key through the lock. Poke it too hard and it would miss the paper, and land with a loud CLANG on the wooden floor. That was sure to alert Aunt Alberta.

This had to be done very slowly.

Little by little the key passed out of the hole. **CLUNK.**

Stella caught it with the sheet of paper below.

Next she pulled the paper back under the door. Her face lit up as she saw the key pass through the gap. She clasped it to her chest as if it was the most precious thing in the world. Her hands shook in anticipation. She put the key back in the lock, and like a master criminal cracking a safe turned it very gently.

CLICK.

The door was unlocked.

The little girl turned the big brass handle and opened the door. At first just a crack. She peeped through the gap, checking that the coast was clear. The long, empty corridor stretched out before her.

Stella was still barefoot and in her nightdress. There wasn't time to dress properly. Alberta might come back to check on her at any moment. She had to make her escape right now, while she still had the chance.

Having lived at Saxby Hall her entire life, Stella knew the house inside out. Without even thinking she was aware of where every creak in the floor was. Tiptoeing along the corridor, she artfully dodged every squeak. Creeping around like this, she felt like a burglar in her own home.

Finally Stella reached the landing, and peered through the balustrades at the top of the stairs. From there she could just see the huge oak front door of Saxby Hall.

When it came to creaks or squeaks the stairs were even more treacherous than the corridor. The little girl descended the first flight with extreme caution.

Halfway down she heard a noise behind her.

CLOMP CLOMP CLOMP.

Footsteps.

CLOMP CLOMP CLOMP.

Someone was coming along the corridor.

CLOMP CLOMP CLOMP.

Stella looked behind her.

CLOMP CLOMP CLOMP.

It was only Gibbon, the butler.

Stella sighed with relief. Much as Stella wanted to beg him to help her escape, it was no use. The faithful manservant was so ancient now he had become almost completely deaf and blind. Try as anyone might, there was absolutely no way of getting through to him. He was in a world all of his own.

Gibbon's black frock coat was dusty and worn, his white serving gloves were riddled with holes, and his old worn shoes flapped whenever he took a step.

However, the butler was marching proudly down the corridor carrying his silver tray. Wobbling on top of it was a tiny pot plant. "Your breakfast, Duchess!" he announced, as he opened the door to a cupboard and stepped inside.

Stella shook her head. The poor old butler was always getting everything wrong.

As quickly and quietly as she could, the girl continued descending the stairs.

SQUEEEEEEAK.

NO! She had forgotten the noisiest stair, the very last one up from the entrance hall. To have come all this way and be caught now would be a disaster.

At the far end of the corridor Stella could hear noises coming from her father's study. It was the sound of the room being ransacked – books and boxes were crashing to the floor, and papers were being scattered. Alberta was talking to herself. She was cursing angrily, "Where have you hidden these blasted deeds?!"

Stella figured that her aunt wouldn't have heard her, and began to tiptoe across the hall to the front door.

RING RING RING RING.

The noise gave the little girl a fright.

RING RING RING RING.

It stopped her in her tracks.

RiNG RiNG RiNG RiNG.

But it was only the telephone
ringing in what was Papa's study.

RiNG RiNG Ri–

Alberta picked it up. Stella stayed dead still to listen.

"Saxby Hall, Lady Saxby speaking!" said the woman.

The girl shook her head in disbelief. Alberta might have
been Lady Alberta, but she wasn't 'Lady Saxby'. That
was Stella's mother's title, and now it was hers.

"Ah, Headmistress! Lovely to hear from you."

It must be Miss Beresford, the headmistress of Stella's
school, St Agatha's School for Aristocratic Girls.

"No, she won't be coming back to St Agatha's any
time soon. There's no change I'm afraid. Yes, she's still
in a very deep coma."

How could her aunt tell a complete and utter lie
like this?

"No, no, there's no need for you or any of the girls to
visit, thank you! I know it's Christmas coming up, but

you can post her present and I will look after it for her. Yes, Headmistress, it is a sad, sad situation. Especially for me as my niece means the world to me. Oh yes, of course, I'll call you the moment she wakes up. If she ever does, that is. Perhaps we all have to prepare ourselves for the worst. I am so sorry, Headmistress, but I am in floods of tears at the thought."

Next came the sound of Alberta wailing.
"Ah-ah-ah! AH-AH-AH!! AAH-AAH-AAH!!! AAAHHH-AAAHHH-AAAHHH!!!!" before she finished the telephone call with a bright and breezy, "Toodle-pip!" DING!

The handset was put back on its hook.

"Nosy old trout," Alberta muttered to herself.

Stella was terrified. *"Prepare ourselves for the worst"*?! What was the wicked woman planning for her? She had to escape. Now.

The girl tiptoed past the ancient suit of armour that always stood by the front door. She was careful not to brush against the suit, or the weapon it was holding in its metal glove – a flail – might fall to the floor. The spiked ball and chain was sure to make a loud

CLANK on the floor if it did.

Silently Stella made her way over to the huge oak front door. She turned the handle, but it was locked. Normally it was only locked from the outside when the family went out, but Alberta had locked it from the inside. Presumably to keep her niece in. Since Stella could remember, the numerous keys for this sprawling country house had all been kept in a cupboard by the door. Stella checked the cupboard. It came as no surprise to find it was bare. Alberta must have hidden all the keys somewhere.

Next the girl clambered up on to the windowsill, and tried to open the windows. They were locked too. Smashing one was far too risky. The noise of shattering glass was sure to alert her aunt, much more than a squeak in the floor.

As Alberta continued her search for the deeds, cursing and emptying boxes in the study, Stella remembered something. Her mama and papa always kept a secret spare key for themselves under the doormat in case of emergency. Stella was pretty sure Alberta wouldn't have known about it. Lifting up the mat, the old rusty key lay there like a piece of long-buried treasure.

As she straightened up holding the key in her hand, Stella slowly realised something. Two large yellow eyes were staring back at her. The eyes of an owl. It was Wagner. He was hanging upside down from a light fitting on the ceiling. Like a bat. A terrifying owly bat.

IX

Hunted Down

If there is one piece of information I hope you take away from this book it's this… You can't reason with a Great Bavarian Mountain Owl.

"O-h-h hello, W-W-W-Wagner…" stuttered Stella. "Don't worry about me, I am just popping out to take in some air."

The owl's two yellow upside-down eyes narrowed.

"S-s-so there's no need to mention this to my lovely aunt!"

"SQUAWK!"

Wagner's squawk was deafeningly loud.

"SQUAWK! SQUAWK! SQUAWK!"

"Shhh…" pleaded the girl.

It was no use. You just can't reason with them.

Soon the monstrous bird was flapping his vast wings, knocking over the ancient suit of armour and sending it, and the flail it was holding in its metal glove, falling to the floor with a mighty

CRASH CLATTER RATTLE!

"Shh…! Shh…! You stupid bird!"

It was almost as if the Great Bavarian Mountain Owl understood what the little girl was saying, because this made Wagner squawk and flap his wings even more violently.

Within moments Stella could hear Aunt Alberta thundering out of the study towards her.

"Wagner," she hooted. **"WAGNER…!"**

Trembling with fear Stella pushed the key into the lock. It rattled around as she frantically tried to turn it.

Out of the corner of her eye Stella could see her aunt getting closer and closer as she made her way along the long corridor. Alberta wasn't a fast runner.

Wrestling was more her kind of sport. However, she was advancing steadily, like a tank.

After what seemed like an hour, but was probably less than a second, the little girl finally heard the click of the lock turning. Fumbling she grabbed the handle, and hurled herself out into the darkness.

The moon was full and low that night. It illuminated the thick covering of snow on the ground. Her feet were moving so fast she could barely feel the cold. As she ran and ran the little girl could just about make out where she was running to. Nonetheless, she nearly

ran straight into the huge snow figure that was being built on the lawn. Up close she realised it had to be at least ten times as tall as her. Looking back over her shoulder, Stella could see her aunt framed in the front doorway, Wagner perched on her hand. The woman was standing still. That she was not chasing after her, frightened Stella. It was as if Aunt Alberta was in complete control.

"BRING ME BACK THAT WRETCHED GIRL!" bellowed the woman, and the

great bird launched himself into the air.

Stella's heart was pounding now. The towering metal gates at the end of the driveway were still a long way ahead of her. Her feet were clawing up with the cold, and now she was stumbling as she ran.

Above her somewhere, Stella could hear the flapping of wings. She looked up at the black sky, but couldn't see where the owl was. The sound of the wings was getting louder and louder. Wagner was getting nearer and nearer.

From the doorway Aunt Alberta was calling out commands to her bird.

"STAY ON COURSE, WAGNER! STAY ON COURSE!"

Stella tried to run faster. She ran faster than she ever had in her life. Tonight it felt like she was running *for* her life. At last she reached the huge iron gates to Saxby Hall. Desperately she pulled at them and they rattled and rattled, but they wouldn't budge. Aunt Alberta must have locked them too. The girl was completely out of breath. Her feet were cramping up. Her skin was burning with the cold. But she still had some fight left in her. *There must be another way out!* she thought. She began running around the perimeter wall. It was tall and made of bricks, but there had to be a hole in it somewhere. Or a tree she could climb so she could jump over into one of the many fields that backed on to Saxby Hall.

"NOW DIVE!"

shouted Alberta.

Stella could hear the great bird speeding through the air behind her. The girl didn't dare look up. She just kept on running. Suddenly her feet weren't touching

the ground any more. Her legs were still moving but now she was flying through the air.

"SQUAWK!"

came a deafening cry in her ear. She looked in terror to see Wagner's razor-sharp talons wrapped around her shoulders. The giant owl had plucked her from the ground as if he were hunting prey.

Stella tried to shake the bird off. Desperately she

lashed out at the fearsome creature with her fists. Wagner suddenly soared higher into the black sky. Stella looked beneath her dangling feet; it was an awfully long way down. If the owl let go now she would plummet to the ground. It was so terrifying Stella scrunched up her eyes as tightly as she could.

Meanwhile, Aunt Alberta watched as the owl circled in the sky, before returning her niece to the house. A sinister smile crossed her face.

X

Locked in the Cellar

"Of course this is just for your own safety, child," lied Aunt Alberta.

The woman had taken her niece down to a tiny, dark coal cellar in the vaults of the house. The walls, floor and ceiling were completely black with coal dust. The cellar was underground, so there were no windows. The only light was from a flickering candle Alberta was holding. Wagner was perched on her other hand. Stella, still barefoot and in her nightdress, had been forced to sit on the floor. Aunt Alberta towered over her niece menacingly.

"You can't lock me up in here!" exclaimed Stella.

"It's only for your own good," replied the woman.

"How can being shut away in a coal cellar be for

my own good?!" The girl's spirit wasn't broken yet.

"Because, child, with your poor mother and father gone, it has fallen to me, your favourite aunty-waunty to looky-wooky after you."

"You are my only auntie!" said the girl.

"Then I must be your favourite! I know their passing must be terribly upsetting for you, as indeed it is to me…"

"You don't seem at all sad about it!" interrupted Stella, but it didn't affect Alberta's flow.

"…but you must never try and run away from home again. Running through the snow barefoot in your nightdress. Good heavens! You could catch your deathy-weathy."

"I need to know the truth of what happened to my parents!" demanded the girl.

Aunt Alberta paused for a moment. Her eyes narrowed. "I told you the truth, young lady. It. Was. An. Accident. **A, C, C, E, D, A, N, T.** * spells accident!" Each word was loud and clipped, coming out of her mouth like bullets being fired from a gun.

"It's a lie!"

"How dare you! Wicked child. Aunt Alberta has never ever ever told a lie."

"You told me all my bones were broken! That was a lie!"

Stella could see the woman was becoming angrier and angrier. Her big, bulbous nose was twitching with fury, but she was trying to hide it.

"They were all broken, child. Every last one. That's why I bandaged you up."

"And you lied on the telephone to my headmistress when you said I was still in a coma!"

---

*Please don't write to me moaning that I can't spell. It's not my fault that Aunt Alberta is pants at spelling. Any letters of complaint should be sent through time directly to her, Ms Alberta Saxby, Saxby Hall, nr Little Saxby, England.

Now Aunt Alberta let out a long low growl.

"Gggggggrrrrrrr!"

This startled the owl, who was perched as always on her hand. Wagner turned his head 180 degrees to see where the sound was coming from. Alberta quickly composed herself. "You had only just woken up, child. You weren't well enough to go back to school straight away. So, yes, perhaps I bent the truth a teeny-weeny bit, but only to protect you, my darling Stella-wella-woo-wah."

Aunt Alberta had an answer for everything. Stella sighed. "I am really hungry. And thirsty."

"Of course you are, you poor dear! Wagner can do one of his special shakes!" said the woman with a flourish.

"Shakes?" asked the girl.

"Yes, like you had when you were in your coma. So nutritious. In fact, I have some very tasty ingredients in my pockets. He can chew them all up for you, so it's in liquid form!"

"No!" protested Stella.

Aunt Alberta started rummaging through her pockets. "What do you fancy?" she asked cheerfully. She pulled out a cockroach and a field mouse. "Cockroach and mouse shake?"

"Noooooooo!" protested the girl.

Aunt Alberta did some more rummaging. "Sparrow and toad drink?"

"Nooooooooo!"

"Or how about a nice worm and mole smoothie?"*

"Nooooooooooooooooo!"

---

*Other shake flavours available included:
Otter & snail; tadpole & vole; chaffinch & caterpillar; bat & spider; frog & wasp; moth & fox cub; hedgehog & centipede; stoat & hornet; eel & grasshopper; grass snake & newt

Wagner was becoming overexcited at seeing all this food, and was bobbing his head and squawking in delight. His mistress dropped a handful of these poor unfortunate creatures into his bill. The owl began swirling them around in his mouth.

"You can have them all together! What a special treat!"

"I think I am going to be sick!" said Stella, covering her mouth.

"There's a bucket in the corner, child. You can do your toilety-woilety in there too. Your poo-poo-poodle-pops and your wee-willy-wee-wees!" The woman turned her attention back to her owl. "Wagner! Swallow." The food slipped down his throat. "There's a good owly-wowly." Alberta kissed him on his bill and trotted over to the metal door.

"You can't leave me here!" protested Stella.

"It's for your own safety, child. We can't have you trying to run away again now, can we?"

"Well, where are you going?" asked the girl.

"I need to find those deeds. They were nowhere to be seen in your father's study. I tried interrogating Gibbon, but the old fool mistook me for a horse. He kept trying to pat me and feed me sugar lumps from his hand saying 'nice horsey'!"

Stella tried to stifle a laugh, as her aunt continued, "I've turned this house upside down looking for those deeds. When your father's will was read, he said he had hidden them somewhere I would never find them. It's absolutely infuriating!" Alberta stamped her feet on the floor in frustration, before she looked down at her trembling niece. "Are you sure you don't know where they are, child?"

"Yes," replied Stella, a little too fast this time.

Alberta could sense the child was lying. "Surely your dear papa would have told his darling daughter?!"

"No." Stella gulped again.

She knew exactly where the deeds were. Her papa had told her his hiding place and it was ingenious. It was somewhere the late Lord Saxby was convinced that his sister Alberta would never ever look.

Can you guess where?

XI

Behind the Walls

The deeds were hidden in *The Tiddlywinks Rulebook*.

In searching for the deeds to Saxby Hall Stella's father Chester was sure his sister would empty the safe, ransack his study, even tear up the floorboards. But she would never ever look there. Of course Aunt Alberta was a dreadful cheat at tiddlywinks. The official rules of the game were of absolutely no

interest to her whatsoever. She had her own rules. Alberta's rules. Rules that she could change on a whim. The book had never even been opened. It was the perfect hiding place for the deeds.

In the coal cellar, Aunt Alberta looked down at her niece.

"Well, Stella, you need to have a good old thinky-winky about where those deeds are hidden."

"I have no idea, Auntie."

"So you keep saying. Perhaps after being left down here alone in the dark for a few days you might just remember. Toodle-pip!"

With that Aunt Alberta slammed the thick metal door behind her, and locked it. This time she took the key out of the lock for safekeeping. She wasn't going to be caught out like that again. Stella listened to the sound of receding footsteps, as her aunt climbed the old stone staircase back into the main part of the house.

Without the light from the candle, the cellar was now pitch-black. It was a pity that Stella was afraid of the dark. Still in just her nightdress, the girl crawled over to where she remembered the door was. Feeling with her hands, she found the handle, but it wouldn't open. It was pointless to even try, but Stella was desperate not to be left down here a moment longer. Next she traced the edges of the room with her fingers, searching for any holes or gaps in the wall she might be able to scratch away at with her fingernails to make bigger. There weren't any. The floor was made of stone, and had to be inches thick.

"Ow!" She banged her head against a metal bucket, and then her hands found a mound of pieces of coal that had been piled up in a corner of the room. Defeated, there was nothing left to do but try and rest. Stella moved the lumps of coal around with her hands in an attempt to make a pillow for her head. Lying there she began to softly cry herself to sleep.

Just as the girl shut her eyes there was a sound. It was the sound of someone or something moving around behind the walls. She had heard the exact same noise before, while drifting off to sleep in her bedroom. Back then, when she still had Mama and Papa, Stella would sometimes become so frightened she would run into their room. There her mother and father would give her a big cuddle, and she would snuggle under the blanket between them. They would gently stroke her hair, and plant tender kisses on her forehead. Papa would tell her it was just a tiny mouse, or the rattles and clanks of the silly old water pipes.

How Stella wished she could run to her parents' bedroom tonight. She would trade anything, all of her future and all of her past, for one last family hug right now.

The sound was becoming louder. That someone or something was on the other side of the wall, but moving nearer and nearer to her. It was far too loud to be a mouse, and there were no hot-water pipes or the like all the way down in the coal cellar. Stella didn't dare breathe. She thought if she didn't move or make a sound she might be safe, and whatever it was might pass. However, her heart was pounding in her chest.

BDUM BDUM BDUM.

It was going to give her away.

BDUM BDUM BDUM.

In the silence of the cellar her heartbeat seemed as loud as thunder.

BDUM BDUM BDUM.

Stella held her breath. Then out of the gloom she heard a voice. A child's voice saying, "'Elp me…"

The girl screamed in terror.

XII

Posho

"AAAAAAAAAAAAARRRR RRRRRRGGGGGGGGGGHH HHHHHHHH!!!!!!!!"

"Oh for bloomin' sake stop screamin'!" said the voice.

This only made Stella scream more.

"AAAAAAAAAAAAAA RRRRRRRRRRrrrrGGG GGGGGGGGGGGGGGGGG HHHHHHHHHHHHHHHHH HHHHHHHH!!!!!!!!!!!!!!"

"Oh shut yer cake 'ole!" It was definitely the voice of a boy. His accent was infinitely rougher around the edges than Stella's.

135

The cellar was pitch-black, and the girl had no idea who she was talking to.

"Who are you?" demanded Stella.

"I'll tell ya, but ya 'ave to promise ya won't scream the place down," he replied.

"Y-y-yes."

"Ya promise?"

"Yes," replied Stella, a little more confidently this time.

"Ready?"

"Yes."

"Ya sure ya won't scream?"

"YES!" Stella was becoming a tiny bit irritated now.

The voice paused for a moment.

"Well, get on with it."

"I am gettin' on wiv it. So, I am a… ghost."

"AAAAAAAAAAAAAAA
AAAAAAAAAAAAAAAAAA
AAAAAAAAAAAAAAAAAA
AAAAAAAAAAAAAAAAAA

RRRRRRRRRRRRRRRrrrrrrrr
RRRRRRRRRRRRRrrrrrrrr
RRRRRRRRRRRRRrrrrrrrrr
GGGGGGGGGGGGGGGGGG
GGGGGGGGGGGGGGGGGGG
GGGGGGGGGGGGGGGGGGG
HHHHHHHHHHHHHHHHH
HHHHHHHHHHHHHHHHH
HHHHHHH!!!" Stella screamed.

The ghost was mightily annoyed. "Ya promised ya weren't gonna scream!"

"Well, I didn't know you were going to say that you were a ghost!" protested the girl.

"Well, wot do ya want me to do? Tell a porky pie?"

"A what?"

"A lie! Cockney rhymin' slang, innit?"

Stella finally understood. "Oh yes."

"What d'ya want me to do? Say I'm Father Christmas or summink?!"

"No, but…" The girl hesitated.

"But wot?"

"You can't be a ghost. Ghosts aren't real! My mama and papa told me so."

The voice replied in a rather smug tone, "Oh did they? 'Mama and papa'!" He chuckled at how posh this girl was. "Very la-de-da! Well if ghosts ain't real, why did ya scream?!"

There was silence for a moment. Stella couldn't think of a reply. Then she said, "I may have been screaming just for fun!"

"Likely story!"

"Well, it's completely dark down here. I can't see you. I can't see a thing! If you really are a ghost, then prove it!" Stella was sure she had him on the ropes now.

"All right!" came the confident reply. "Shift some of this 'ere coal out the way."

"Me?!" asked the girl incredulously. Despite not having any money, Stella had enjoyed a privileged upbringing as a member of the upper class. Being posh, she was not used to being given orders. Especially not to move lumps of coal about. And especially not in such an uncouth manner by someone so clearly of the lower classes who her rather grand headmistress might have charitably described as an 'oik'.*

"Yeah! You!" the ghost replied. It was clear he was having none of this girl's attitude, but she wasn't giving up yet.

"Well, why can't you do it?" she said defiantly. By the sound of the ghost's rough accent, Stella was sure moving coal around the floor of a cellar was much more his kind of thing. In fact, she guessed he would probably love to do it. For him it would actually be a pleasure, an honour; perhaps even something of a treat. Maybe if this were his birthday, giving him the opportunity to move some coal about would make the perfect present.

"I'm stuck the other side of it in this 'ere coal chute, ain't I? I ain't got no place to shift it to."

"Well, you are a ghost aren't you?"

A lout, a ruffian, an urchin.

"DUH! Yeah!"

"So, can't you just, well, 'waft' through it?"

"Nah. Real ghosts can't 'waft'."

Stella's understanding of ghosts came purely from fanciful stories she had read. She was more than a little disappointed to learn that real ghosts could not walk through walls after all. Not least because it meant she had to move this mountain of coal by herself.

"Sorry, I had no idea," she said. Yet the girl stood totally still, hoping that if she did nothing for long enough this 'oik' would do it for her anyway. However, this was not to be.

"Come on!" the ghost moaned. "The quicker ya get started the quicker ya finish."

Stella sighed, and bent down to feel where the coal was on the stone floor of the cellar. Reluctantly she started moving pieces aside. It was hard work, and when she paused for a moment to get her breath back the ghost shouted, "Get a move on!"

"I am going as fast as I can!" protested Stella.

"Sorry, but moving coal around is not something I normally do."

The ghost let out a chuckle. "Nah! Yer one of dem Poshos!"

"What? I mean I beg your pardon?"

"Posho!" The ghost seemed to really enjoy saying the word and started to tease her with it. "POSHO! POSHO! POSHO!" It was all very childish, but then he was a child. Well, the ghost of a child.

"I am not a 'posho'!" exclaimed the girl, more than a little offended.

"Na! Course yer not."

"Thank you."

"Now come on, Posho! Put yer back into it! Ha ha!"

Now I know what you are thinking: why haven't there been any illustrations in this chapter? The pictures are the best bit. Well, that's because the last few pages of

the story have taken place completely in the dark.
In case you feel cheated, here are some illustrations
especially for you.

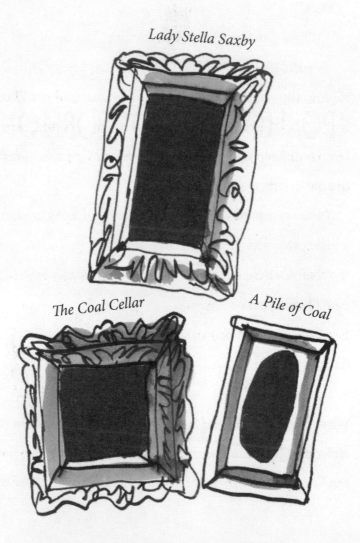

Lady Stella Saxby

The Coal Cellar

A Pile of Coal

XIII

A Light in the Shape of a Boy

There was no point Stella arguing with the ghost. The little girl sighed and went back to work. Groping with her hands in the dark, she continued moving the lumps of coal across the cellar floor.

After a while she could see something glowing. At first she couldn't make out what it was, but as she moved more coal out of the way she realised it was a pair of feet. Dirty-looking feet that were somehow lighting up the cellar. Now she could see what she was doing, the  girl quickened her pace. Soon all the coal had been pushed aside and standing right in front of her was a light in the shape of a boy.

The figure was wearing shorts, a shirt, and his outfit was topped off with a cap. Over his shoulder he was holding a brush. He had clearly been a chimney sweep, a boy who in the olden days was sent to crawl up chimneys to brush away the coal dust. Now presumably his full-time occupation was 'ghost'.

"Well, that took ya a while!" he said with a cheeky smile.

Stella couldn't believe her eyes. She had been right all along. Those noises she had heard in the middle of the night were a ghost. Saxby Hall really was haunted. Here was the living proof. Well, dead proof.

"You're quite short for a ghost," mused Stella.

"Oh that's nice, innit? Been hidin' meself away for donkey's…"

"Donkeys?" The girl was confused.

"Donkey's ears. Years."

"Oh."

"So I been hiding away cos I didn't wanna frighten nobody, and the first person I meet says I'm a short-arse!"

"Sorry," replied Stella, not quite meaning it.

"Nah, nah, you've said it now, ain't ya? I heard ya cryin' and it made me sad. I thought I might be able to 'elp."

"I wasn't crying really. I just had something in my eye," replied the girl, trying to sound as grown-up as possible. "But that is kind of you. Let's try and be friends." She offered out her hand slowly. "My name is Lady Stella Saxby of Saxby Hall."

"Ooh! La-de-da and la-de-day!" The ghost was most amused, and began to mimick the girl's upper-class voice. "Charmed I am sure, Lady Posho of Posho Hall in Poshington!" Next he began doffing his cap in a manner so over-the-top there was little doubt he was only pretending to be impressed.

Stella observed this display, a pained grin on her face. "So what is your name?"

"Soot."

"No, I asked you what your name is, not what you sweep away."

"I know. It's Soot."

"Soot? That's your name?"

"Yeah."

The girl couldn't help but laugh. "That's not a proper name! You can't be called Soot!"

The ghost didn't look at all pleased at the girl's response. "That's it! Have a good ol' laugh, m'lady!"

"I will!" she replied, before bursting into hysterics.

"Ha ha ha!"

Soot folded his arms, waiting for this rude little madam to stop. "Ya all finished?"

"Yes!" replied Stella, wiping a tear of laughter from her eye. "So, please tell me, how does one end up being called – " she was trying not to giggle "– Soot?!"

"It ain't my fault. I was never given a name. I was abandoned as a baby, and grew up in a workhouse. I never knew me mum or dad. The old man who run the workhouse used to thrash all us boys wiv his belt."

"No!"

"Yeah, even when we ain't done nuffink. So I ran away. I was still only little, and I met a gang of boys on the streets. They said ya could get food and lodgings if ya worked as a chimney sweep. So that's what I did. And one day I came down from the chimney covered from head to toe in coal dust, and me master just called me 'Soot'!"

Now the girl felt very guilty for having laughed. This poor boy's experience of life had been a world away from hers. Stella had never seen inside a workhouse, and shuddered to think how brutal it could be. As for being shoved up a chimney to clean out the coal dust, that was unimaginable. "I am so sorry," she said. "I didn't mean to laugh, it's just that I never ever heard of anyone being called 'Soot'."

"Don't ya worry m'lady."

Stella now had a question she wasn't at all sure how to phrase. "So, um, I hope you don't mind me asking."

"Spit it out!"

"How did you er, well, you know, come to be a ghost?"

Soot looked at her and shook his head. He clearly thought that was an absolutely stupid thing to ask. "You 'ave to die first, don't ya?"

"Yes, yes, I gathered that," replied the girl. "So erm, forgive me, but how did you come to be erm…?"

"Brown bread?"

"Brown bread, rhymes with… dead!" Stella guessed.

"Yer gettin' it!" The pair shared a smile. "Well, m'lady, you may not believe me, but I died in this very house…"

XIV

Ghost Snot

Down in the darkness of the cellar, Stella stood silently listening to Soot's real-life **horror** story.

"It was a very long time ago now," said the ghost. "I was so little me master thought he could push me up any chimney, whatever the size. He knew this house had this maze of chimneys and little tunnels, so I was the perfect lad for the job. Weird fing was I had this really funny feelin' when I walked in the door…" Soot became lost in thought. The light from his body cast shadows on the walls of the cellar. The shadows moved and danced as he spoke, painting pictures from his story like illustrations in a book.

"What do you mean 'a funny feeling'?" Stella was intrigued.

The ghost pondered for a moment. "Dunno, like I'd been here before or summink. But I couldn't 'ave, could I?"

Stella searched her mind for an answer. As he had been abandoned as a baby and grown up in a workhouse, it seemed impossible that he had ever set foot in a great country house before. "I wouldn't have thought so," she replied.

"Nah. I suppose yer right m'lady. Still it was weird. So me master pushed me up the chimney and I was doing me brushin' wiv me oojamaflip…"

"Brush?"

"Yep wiv me brush. Me master had gone out for a smoke. Then Lord love a duck I noticed me bum was getting really 'ot!"

"Hot?" asked the girl.

"Yeah, that's what I said. 'Ot. I looked down the chimney, and someone had only gone and lit the fire."

"Oh no," replied Stella. She felt for the poor boy. "Who could have done that?"

"Dunno. I never saw 'em. I cried for 'elp but no one came runnin'. I guess they couldn't have known I was up there. Before I could say 'Jack Sprat' there was all this smoke coming up. The chimney was so blocked I couldn't climb up it. I was stuck. I was a gonner."

"That's a horrible story…" The little girl was

imagining the whole scene in her mind. Of the hundreds
of ways someone might die, this was particularly
horrifying. Being trapped in a tiny space as thick black
smoke enveloped you. A tear welled up
in her eye, and traced a line down
her coal-blackened face.

"Yer cryin' again, m'lady. I
don't like to see a pretty girl like
ya cry."

Somehow this made Stella cry
more. She cried for Soot, her parents, and finally for
herself.

"And that's me story, m'lady," said Soot.

The little girl dabbed her eyes with her nightdress,
and took a deep breath to gather herself together. "So
why did you stay here at Saxby Hall?"

"I didn't have nowhere else to go, did I?" replied
the ghost. "Didn't have a home, didn't even have a
name, did I? So I couldn't even try to find me family
in that place up in the clouds they tell ya all about in

church. So I just stayed here. Going up and down the chimneys all night."

"I knew Saxby Hall was haunted!" exclaimed the girl. "But my mother and father didn't believe me."

Soot smiled. "Well, the thing with grown-ups is they can't see us ghosts."

"No?" The girl was intrigued.

"Nah! When ya grow up ya stop believin' in magic and all that. So ya can't see anyfink that isn't really there any more. Yer mind has to be open, like a child's. How old are ya, m'lady?"

"I am nearly thirteen." Stella was very proud of this fact, and like most children longed to be older than she was. Sometimes she would dream of being sixteen or eighteen or twenty-one. She would imagine all the things she could do when she was grown-up – drive a car, have a glass of champagne, stay up until dawn.

"Oh dear. Oh dear, oh deary me," said Soot, shaking his head.

"What?"

"When's yer actual birthday, m'lady? I need to know the date."

"My birthday is Christmas Eve. And what is the date today?"

What with the crash, and falling into a coma, the girl had unsurprisingly lost all track of time.

"I am pretty sure it's the twenty-first of December today. So you'll be thirteen in just three days."

"Yes. And that's good, isn't it?" asked the girl.

"No, m'lady. Ya can see me all right now, yer still just a child, but when ya turn thirteen it'll all change."

"I don't believe you!" said Stella sharply.

"There ya go!" retorted the ghost. "Yer still only twelve and already saying ya don't believe in summink!"

"B-b-but..."

"'Scuse me..." With that Soot put a finger up one of his nostrils, and blew on the other. A globule of glowing mucus landed on the floor. The girl had been brought up to be lady. To use the correct cutlery at mealtimes, to ask to be excused from the table, and to blow her nose on a lace handkerchief. She had never seen such disgusting manners.

"Do you mind?" she said, rather offended.

"Keep yer hair on, m'lady, it's only a bit of ghost snot!"

With that he changed nostrils, and blew another globule on to the floor.

"That's revolting!" complained Stella. "Do you not own a handkerchief?!"

"A wot?"

"Clearly not! And now there's ghost snot all over the floor of the cellar, and I am not wearing any shoes!"

Soot stared straight at the girl. "Look, m'lady, it was awful nice to meet ya and all that mullarky, but I don't fink us two are ever gonna be friends. The boys I grew up wiv in the workhouse weren't bothered by a tiny bit of snot."

"It's hardly tiny!" protested Stella.

"In fact there was much worse than that all over the floor in there."

"I shudder to think!"

"One boy dropped his trousers and did an almighty—!"

"I don't need to know, thank you!" replied Stella, cutting the boy off.

Soot looked at Stella. There was an ocean of difference between them that seemed impossible to cross. "I fink it's best we say goodbye." With that the ghost turned around to disappear back up the coal chute.

"Wait!" pleaded the girl. "Please!"

"What now, m'lady?" sighed Soot.

"I need your help."

XV

The Ghost Detective

Climbing up a coal chute was not something Stella had ever imagined herself doing. However, right now the new Lady Saxby was doing just that, following the chimney sweep up out of the cellar. Soot lit the way with his ghostly glow, pointing out where all the bricks that jutted out were, that she could use to hold on to. The ghost knew every nook and cranny of Saxby Hall's endless network of tunnels. The chute was used to deliver bags of coal down to the cellar, where it was stored before it was used in all the fireplaces in Saxby Hall. At the top of the long chute was a small hatch in the wall, leading out to the kitchen.

Climbing up the chute was hard work, especially for young Stella who was tired and hungry. Just as she was

making good progress, her fingers slipped on a piece of damp brickwork.

"Aaah!" cried the girl, as she fell down the chute, sending debris falling. She bounced off the sides, finally managing to stop herself by clinging on with one hand to a tiny piece of brick that was jutting out.

"Don't look down, m'lady!" shouted Soot from above.

Stella couldn't help herself. Immediately she looked down and saw how far up she still was. If she lost her grip she would drop like a stone, and no doubt break both her legs.

"I can't do this any more!" she shouted up in frustration.

"Yes ya can, m'lady. Don't look down."

"I am not looking down!" she protested.

"Reach for that next piece of brick. It's just up to ya left."

"I am going to fall."

"Yer not goin' to fall," reassured the ghost. "Feel for that piece of brick wiv yer hand. 'Ave ya found it?"

The girl reached out her free hand above her. "Yes. I think so."

"Now pull yerself up."

"I haven't got the strength."

"You 'ave, m'lady. I know it. Ya don't want to be left to rot in that coal cellar, do ya?"

"No," mumbled the girl. It was a little like she was being told off. Stella took a deep breath, and pulled herself up.

"There! Ya can do it!" exclaimed Soot. Step by step he guided her up the chute.

Looking up past Soot, Stella could see the patch of light above becoming larger and larger. Eventually she had hoisted herself up to the top of the chute, and clambered out of the hole. Shaken and exhausted, the girl landed in an undignified heap on the cold kitchen floor.

Some of Stella's happiest memories were from this room. Having grown up with an army of servants, her mother had simply never been taught to cook. However, once the staff had to be let go after Alberta had squandered all the family's money, Mama was forced to try. Her cooking was atrocious; it became the stuff of legend. Yet all those cakes that never rose, or jellies that never set, or pancakes that were tossed into the air and got stuck on the ceiling were made with that most important of ingredients, love. The young Stella would help her mother in the kitchen. Together they would make scones for Papa, his absolute favourite.

Even though they would come out of the oven looking like gargoyles, once the scones had been heaped high with huge dollops of clotted cream and raspberry jam, they were absolutely yummy. When her parents were alive the kitchen had always been such a happy place. Sadly now, like so much of the house, it had become deserted.

Sitting on the floor together, Stella told her new friend all about the events that had led up to her being locked in the coal cellar. How she had been in a terrible car crash that cost her parents their lives, a crash she had no memory of whatsoever. How she had been in a coma for months. How her Aunt Alberta was trying to keep her captive in the house. How the evil woman was desperate to find the deeds to Saxby Hall so Stella would have to sign everything over to her. How if she did that she feared for her life, who knows what wickedness her aunt had in store for her? How she had tried to flee to the nearest village, but the giant owl had captured her and brought her back. How there must be more to the tragic 'accident' that killed her parents. How all this pointed the finger of suspicion at Aunt Alberta.

Soot listened to everything the girl said with interest, and when she had finished he thought for a moment. "It is all very fishy, m'lady," he said. "But if ya want the old moo locked up ya need proof."

"Yes, I suppose I do," agreed the girl. "Let's become detectives – just like in my favourite books!" A bolt of energy passed through Stella's body at the thought, and she leaped excitedly to her feet.

"Real-life detectives!" Soot was becoming excited now too.

"And if we work together, we can look for clues. Now where do you think we should start?"

The ghost thought for a moment. "The garage! Find out what 'appened to the car."

"Let's go, Detective Soot!"

"Right ya are, Detective m'lady!"

XVI

A Bitter Aftertaste

To Stella's astonishment, inside the garage sat the family's beautiful Rolls Royce. Except it wasn't beautiful any more. The car was now a jumble of broken glass and twisted metal. The windscreen was smashed, and the bonnet had been squashed to pieces.

The silver-lady statuette that stood proudly above the engine on all Rolls Royces was bent over to one side. In the months since the accident the car had become coated in a thick layer of dust. A spider had even spun a cobweb in one of the broken windows.

Stella wept a river of tears upon seeing the car like this. It made everything real. There really had been a horrific car crash, and judging by the extent of the damage Stella was extremely lucky to be alive. Anyone sitting on the front seats would have been killed in an instant.

"I'm so sorry, m'lady," whispered Soot. Spotting an oily rag on the floor, he bent down to pick it up. "'Ere, wipe yer eyes on this. I know it's not one of yer posh lacy 'andkerchiefs, but it's the best I can do."

Stella was touched by his kindness, and took it with a smile. "Maybe I was wrong to doubt my aunt, she must be telling the truth about the accident," said the girl. She sniffed as she wiped her face, which was now a mess of tears, coal and soot.

"Why lock ya down in the coal cellar if the old witch has nuffink to hide?"

"She said it was for my own good," reasoned Stella. "So I wouldn't try running away again in the middle of the night."

The ghost shook his head. "It smells very fishy to me, m'lady. Now fink. Can ya 'member anyfink about the crash?" he asked. "Anyfink at all?"

The girl searched her mind. "It's all such a blur."

"Anyfink?" insisted Soot. "Don't have to be summink big. Anyfink. Summink small might give us a great big clue to solvin' the case." The ghost was really sounding like a detective now.

Stella thought for a moment, before retracing the events of that day in her mind. "Papa and Mama and I were going to motor down to London. Papa had to go to the bank again. You see my aunt had got us all into terrible debt, and Papa is..." The girl stopped herself for a moment as Soot offered her a supportive smile. "I mean Papa was so charming and clever he always managed to persuade the bank manager to let us keep Saxby Hall. And Mama knew I wanted to see Buckingham Place where the King lives. We never had any money to go inside anywhere. But I didn't mind. I loved my mama so much it never mattered what we did, just as long as we were together, my arm tucked into hers."

"Yer old ma must 'ave been a very special lady," murmured Soot.

For a moment the pair stood in the garage in a sad silence, as the sound of a snowstorm swirled outside.

"She was," Stella agreed eventually. She'd never have thought that the former Lady Saxby would be described as 'yer old ma', but she knew Soot meant it nicely.

"Wot about yer aunt? Did she come wiv ya?" asked the boy.

The girl shook her head. "Papa asked her if she wanted to come, but she said no. Sometimes she would want a ride into London to buy toys for her pet owl to rip to shreds, but not that day."

"That bird gives me the willies!" exclaimed Soot. "He's 'ad a good peck at me over the years. Chased me up chimneys quite a few times."

"They say animals can sense ghosts," said Stella.

"It's more than sense, m'lady. He can see me as clear as day. All animals can. So why didn't yer aunt come too?"

"Oh yes. Well Alberta was very sure she wanted to stay at home."

"Interestink. Very interestink." The ghost was rubbing his chin now, taking to this sleuthing role perfectly. "So do ya 'member anything at all about the crash?"

"No," replied the girl. "Nothing at all. The last thing I recall was feeling very ill and passing out on the back seat of the Rolls."

The ghost had been pacing up and down the garage, but now stopped dead still. This sounded like an important clue. "Ill, m'lady?"

"Yes, I was feeling sick, and I was sweating even though it was a cold day."

"Go on."

"As we motored into town I kept on closing my eyes. The last time I closed them, that's when the Rolls must have crashed."

"Wot about yer ma and pa?"

The girl's mind was racing. It was all coming back to her. "Mama told me she didn't feel well either, but she knew that Papa's meeting with the bank manager was very important. He had to save Saxby Hall. She didn't want him to have to turn back for her."

Soot was convinced they were on to something now. "Wot about yer pa?"

"I don't know," replied the girl with a sigh. "If he wasn't feeling well, he hid it. But that's what Papa was like. He always kept a stiff upper lip."

The ghost began pacing up and down again, trying to put all the pieces of the puzzle together. "If yer old man was feelin' ill too, that could explain the crash."

"I know," agreed the girl. "Sitting on the back seat I kept feeling like I was blacking out."

"Wot could make ya all ill like that?" said Soot, almost to himself. "Was there a funny smell of anyfink in the car?"

"A funny smell? Like what?"

"Dunno. Fumes from the exhaust maybe? That could make you all feel ill."

"No." The girl was certain of that. "There was never anything wrong with the car. It was Papa's pride and joy. He always kept the Rolls in mint condition. The engine purred like a cat when he drove it."

"Then if it's not the car," muttered the ghost, "there must be summink else. Did ya all 'ave anyfink strange to eat dat mornin'?"

"No. Mama cooked us boiled eggs with soldiers. We had that for breakfast every day." Suddenly Stella remembered something. "But…"

"Yeah?" The ghost seized upon this.

"Well, Aunt Alberta made us all a pot of tea that morning."

"A pot of tea?"

"Yes. And she never made us tea. She would never normally do anything like that for us ever. That's why I remembered it. And I remember saying to Mama that the tea tasted funny…"

"Funny?"

"Well, I mean funny peculiar. Strange. But Mama told me to drink it up, so as not to be rude to Alberta. I couldn't stomach it though, so when nobody was looking I poured my cup out into a plant pot."

"Wot did it taste like, m'lady?" asked Soot.

Stella was desperately trying to remember. "I must have only had a mouthful. Bitter somehow. I put lashings of milk and sugar in my tea, but it definitely had a bitter aftertaste."

"Did yer aunt 'ave any of her tea?"

"No. No. She didn't." Stella was sure of it. "Aunt Alberta poured out a cup from the pot for herself, but she never had a sip."

"Did yer ma and pa fink it tasted funny too?"

"Well, if they did they were too polite to say so in front of her," replied Stella. "But I noticed them both grimace when they drank it." Suddenly a thought raced across her mind like a bolt of lightning. "Alberta must have laced the tea with…"

The pair looked at each other and spoke at the same time.

"POISON!"

XVII

Desserts Galore

CRASH!

At that moment, the garage doors smashed open.

"AAAHHHH!" Stella took a sharp intake of breath.

Was there someone or something out there?

There was a blizzard raging outside, and snow swirled inside. Stella ran to the doors, and with all her weight battled to fight the strong gusts of wind. Soot followed her, and together they managed to close and bolt them shut.

"There's no way ya can try and run away again tonight, m'lady," said the ghost. "You'll have to wait until the storm dies down. But for now it looks like it's here to stay."

Panic flashed across the little girl's face. "But I don't dare wait another moment. My aunt has already tried to poison me and Mama and Papa, who knows what she will try next?! I have to call the police!"

"Don't ya fink we need some more evidence first?" suggested Soot.

"No! I have to call right now!" exclaimed the girl. "But it's very dangerous."

"Why?"

"There are only two telephones in the house. One in Alberta's room, but she keeps the door locked at all times. The other is in Papa's study, and my aunt is convinced the deeds to Saxby Hall are in there. She is spending day and night in that study, turning the whole place upside down."

Soot thought for a moment. "Maybe I can try and cause a diversion."

"Like what?"

"Oh I dunno. Throw some plates around? Us ghosts love doin' stuff like that. It normally works a treat."

"But what if you get caught?" asked Stella. In the short time she had known this little chimney sweep, she had become rather fond of him.

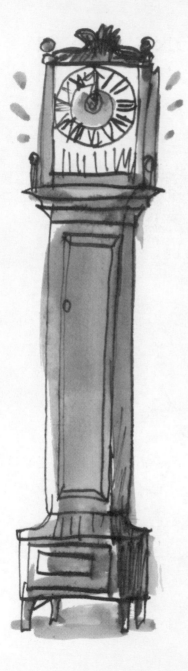

"Aunt Alberta is a grown-up, she's not going to be able to see me, is she?"

"Yes of course," replied the girl, still struggling to remember all these ghost rules. "What about Wagner?"

"We'll have to pray he is sleeping. That is one scary owl!"

Stella and Soot tiptoed along the corridor. The grandfather clock gave them both a fright, as it chimed midnight.

BONG!
BONG!
BONG!
BONG!

BONG! BONG! BONG! BONG! BONG! BONG! BONG! BONG!

Soon they reached the entrance to the grand dining room. They peeked their heads around the open door and saw Alberta and Wagner enjoying a midnight feast. No doubt the woman thought her niece was still safely locked up in the coal cellar where she had left her. How could she have known that Stella was in fact just a few steps away.

The woman sat at one end of the endless dining table, her pet owl was perched at the other, a napkin tied around his neck. A huge candelabrum with twenty or so candles burning on it illuminated the room.

The table was piled high with desserts – that's all Aunt Alberta ever ate. She never had a main course. Or a starter. No, Aunt Alberta went straight to the pudding. She would scoff desserts for breakfast, lunch and dinner, which was why she was as wide as she was tall.

There were desserts galore!

– A giant apple strudel, made from at least a hundred apples.

– A towering pyramid of chocolate balls.

– Eclairs the size of pillows.

– A huge chocolate cake oozing with buttercream.

– Cream puffs piled up to the ceiling.

– A trifle so big you could swim in it.

– Deep-fried doughnuts pumped full of jam.

– A mouth-watering Black Forest gateau. You only

had to look at it to double your body weight.

– A huge vat of salted caramel, still bubbling from the stove.

– A life-sized owl made entirely of marzipan.

– A deep bucket of cream that had a huge dollop of cream on top for good measure.

– All-butter biscuits that had been double dipped in chocolate.

– A wobbly jelly so ginormous it could break the fall of a hippopotamus.

Stella's mouth watered when she saw all this glorious food. The poor girl hadn't eaten for days. For a moment she thought she might faint at the sweet smell of it all. Aunt Alberta was tucking in greedily, making loud slurping noises…

"SLURP!"

…and belching between mouthfuls.

"BURP!"
"BUUUURPPP!"
"BUUUUUUUURR RPPPPPPPP!!!"

Alberta could have won bronze, silver and gold at the Burping Olympics.

Meanwhile Wagner was helping himself from a cold buffet of dead woodland creatures. There were mice, squirrels, hedgehogs, sparrows, even a badger. All his favourite treats.

As the woman ate she sifted through a large box of papers from the study, hurling documents angrily over her shoulder.

"Where are those blasted deeds?" she muttered to herself, between gobbling down huge mouthfuls of Black Forest gateau.

"Come on, m'lady," whispered Soot. The girl had become mesmerised by the cakes.

The pair sank down to their hands and knees, and crawled past the door.

The very next room was Papa's study. Stella's father had always kept the room in perfect order. It was Lord Saxby's little sanctuary. Now documents, photographs, boxes, folders and books were strewn across the floor. The desk had been upturned, glass smashed on the cabinets, and Papa's large leather chair had been ripped open with a knife. It was as if a bomb had exploded in there. Aunt Alberta had clearly been looking EVERYWHERE for the deeds.

The telephone usually sat on the desk, but now the study had been ransacked it was nowhere to be seen. Stella went over to the wall and found the end of the cable. Then she traced her hand along it until she found the telephone, hiding under a huge pile of papers. With the telephone safely sat on her lap Stella signalled over to Soot, who was waiting just outside in the corridor keeping a lookout.

"Go!" she whispered.

"Wot?" replied Soot.

"Go!" she said, louder this time.

The ghost nodded, and went off to create his diversion. It was to be a pretty standard ghost-throwing-plates-around-the-kitchen routine, but hopefully enough to make Alberta come running and win Stella some time.

You may be interested to know that the spookiest tricks favoured by the British Society of Poltergeists (BSP) include:

– Knocking on doors and running away.

– Putting records on the player and turning the volume dial up very loud.

– Hurling books around in the library.

– Pushing over large items of furniture.

– Jangling chains in the middle of the night.

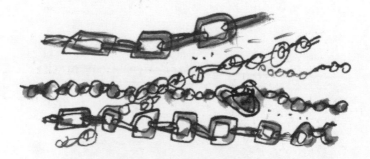

– Making two chairs dance together.

– Levitating the cutlery.

– Flushing the toilet when
someone is still sitting on it.

– Prancing around the
bedroom with a bedsheet
on the head.

– Moving objects around the house randomly, such as putting someone's underpants in the fridge.

– Doing an evil laugh into a jar, to make it echo around a house.

– Drawing a rude picture of a bottom on the bathroom mirror and waiting for the mirror to steam up for it to be revealed.

If any of these have happened to you, perhaps your house is haunted. Or it could be just your annoying little brother.

The girl listened as far along the corridor plates started crashing on to the floor of the kitchen. Within moments Stella could hear Aunt Alberta shouting, **"Wagner! Wagner!"** from the next room. Then there was the unmistakeable sound of the large woman thundering down the corridor.

This was Stella's chance.

She had to take it.

Now.

Right now.

XVIII

Crackle Crackle Crackle

Stella crouched in her father's study, and took a deep breath. She lifted the telephone receiver and placed it to her ear. The girl wasn't sure she could hear a dialling tone, there was so much noise coming from the kitchen. Still she put her finger in the dial and turned it. The girl winced at the loud whirring noise of the dial returning to its place, despite all the hullabaloo from down the corridor. As she heard plate after plate smashing to the ground, Stella turned the dial twice more, and waited anxiously. Finally a voice came on the other end of the line.

"Hello?" came an unusually high-pitched tone. "Emergency Services. What service do you require please?"

"Police!" replied Stella as quickly and quietly as she could.

"I am sorry, miss, could you repeat that? There is a loud noise your end."

"Yes, yes, of course, I am sorry," said the girl, speaking louder this time. "I need the police, right away."

"The police! Putting you through."

There was a pause, then another voice came on the line. A much deeper one – so deep it was almost a **growl**.

"Police here. Little Saxby Police Station. What crime are you reporting, miss?"

"It is a, erm…" Somehow Stella felt foolish saying it.

"Go on," prompted the voice.

"It's a…"

"Yes? Spit it out!"

"A murder!" There. She'd said it.

On the other end of the line there was silence for a moment, before the voice asked, "A murder?"

"Yes!" replied the girl. "In fact two murders!"

"Any more?"

Stella was more than a little taken aback by the policeman's tone. Perhaps he thought it was another stupid child making a hoax call.

"Look, you must believe me, sir," pleaded Stella, "I am deadly serious. Yes just two. Well, not 'just' two. Two! Two is still a lot."

"So you are sticking at two?"

"Yes."

"Just the two murders?"

"That's right, yes."

"Any advance on two?"

"No."

"So, miss, would you care to tell me who exactly has been murdered?"

"Mama and Papa. I mean my mother and father."

"You're sure?"

"Yes."

"Interesting. So who do you believe did the actual murdering?"

Stella hesitated for a moment before replying, "My aunt."

"I am sorry, I couldn't hear what you said, I think there must be a problem on the line because I thought you said your 'aunt'!"

Next Stella had to remove the receiver from her ear, as there was a deafening crackle on the other end.

CRACKLE CRACKLE CRACKLE.

"Repeat that please?" demanded the voice.

"That's right, sir. I did say my aunt."

"Sorry, this must be a very bad line."

CRACKLE CRACKLE CRACKLE.

"It's my aunt!" exclaimed Stella, a little louder than she should have. "Her name's Alberta. Alberta Saxby."

There was a scribbling sound on the other end of the line as if the policeman was making notes. "So you did say your aunt. This Alberta Saxby, is she a Miss a Mrs or a Ms?"

"Ms I think."

"Ms?"

"Yes, Ms."

"Ms Alberta Saxby." It was clear the policeman was taking notes. "Now I hardly need to tell you that there is a terrible snowstorm all over England tonight."

"Yes, I know," replied Stella. She could hear the snow tapping on the window of the study as they spoke.

"So, miss, I am afraid this is going to have to wait until the morning."

Stella felt scared. Who knew what the wicked woman might do to her before then? "Are you sure you can't send anyone tonight? Please!" she pleaded.

"Quite sure, miss," came the firm reply. "But rest assured, as this is a murder, a double murder, beg your pardon, miss, we shall send our best detective from the police headquarters at Scotland Yard in London first thing in the morning. Goodbye."

Just as she was about to put down the receiver, Stella remembered something. "Don't you need my address?"

"Oh yes!" said the voice on the other end. "I do beg your pardon, miss. What is your address please?"

"It's Saxby Hall."

"Saxby Hall, yes, I have that all down now. And sorry I don't think I got your name, miss?"

"Well, I am, in fact..."

"Yes?"

Stella eventually blurted out, "Lady Saxby." She knew from being with her parents that using your title always made other people sit up and take notice.

"A Lady! Are you indeed?" The tone sounded a little mocking.

"Erm, yes. I am the new Lady Saxby. Lady Stella Saxby."

"Well, 'Lady' Saxby, it is awfully late now, the clock here on station wall says it's well after midnight. It must be way past your bedtime."

"Yes, yes it is," agreed Stella, although it seemed impossible to even think about going to sleep right now.

"Then I suggest you go straight to bed, and the detective will be with you first thing in the morning."

"You promise?"

"I promise, miss, beg your pardon, 'Lady' Saxby. First thing."

"Thank you." Stella just had to try and stay alive until then.

"And Lady Saxby?"

"Yes?" asked the girl.

"Don't have nightmares."

CLICK.

The voice was gone.

XIX

Deeply Creepy

Stella put down the receiver and tiptoed slowly out of Papa's study, back along the corridor. With great caution she approached the kitchen. Dinner plates, cups, saucers and bowls were all flying out of cupboards and smashing on the floor. The kitchen was becoming almost knee-deep in broken crockery.

Wagner zoomed around the kitchen chaotically, this way and that, trying to peck at the ghost with his razor-sharp bill. As Stella walked in Soot was fighting the bird off with a gravy boat, before that too went hurtling to the floor, exploding into hundreds of pieces.

To the little girl's surprise, Aunt Alberta was nowhere to be seen. Stella panicked, perhaps the woman had rushed down to the cellar to check on her?

So without being seen by Wagner, Stella tiptoed through the broken crockery, and over to the coal chute.

Just as she had climbed inside, her eyes peeping out of the top, Aunt Alberta burst into the room. The woman looked utterly confused as to what was going on. **"Wagner!"** she shouted. "The crockery! What are you doing to the crockery! Bad bird!"

It was clear to Stella that Soot was right, grown-ups couldn't see ghosts. Rather deliciously, Alberta was blaming her pet owl for all the damage.

The way down the coal chute was harder than the way up. Without Soot's ghostly light to guide her, it was a terrifying journey downwards in total darkness. At any moment Stella thought she might fall. Eventually her bare feet touched the cold stone floor. Just as they did so, Stella could hear loud footsteps running down the stairs. It was her aunt coming to check on her! As quickly as she could, Stella lay down on the cellar floor and closed her eyes, pretending to be asleep. She heard the jangling of keys, then the great steel door was unlocked and slowly creaked open. The girl kept her eyes shut and even attempted a little light snoring to sell the idea that she had been fast asleep for hours.

Zzzz
Zzzz
Zzzzz.

It was a deeply creepy feeling, sensing her aunt moving around her in the cellar.

For a moment all was still, and Stella could smell the damp leather of Alberta's boots. She couldn't resist opening one eye the tiniest bit. Out of the slit of her eye she spied a huge black boot staring back at her.

It couldn't be any closer to her face. As quickly as she could she shut her eye again. Stella was sure she had given the game away. She could sense the slight flicker of warmth from a candle as it was brought down to her face. All the same she kept deadly still, and soon she heard her aunt's footsteps moving back to the cellar door. Even now Stella waited, until she heard the door being locked, and the footsteps going back up the stairs. Then she opened her eyes again. The girl breathed a huge sigh of relief. She had convinced her aunt she had been asleep all along.

Stella sat up on the cold stone cellar floor. It was a world away from her comfy old four-poster bed upstairs. Then she heard a scratching sound coming from the coal chute. Next a light glowed dimly in the cellar, before it became brighter and brighter.

It was Soot!

Never did Stella think she would be so happy to see a ghost.

"So, m'lady, did ya make yer call on the old dog and bone?" he asked.

"The what?"

"The telephone!"

"Oh yes!" She was still new at this Cockney rhyming slang malarkey. "Yes, I called the police, they are sending their best detective from Scotland Yard first thing in the morning."

"That's tops!" exclaimed Soot. "Well, m'lady, ya try and get some sleep. Ya need to be ready to tell that copper everyfink in the mornin'."

"You're right."

"Now I'll climb up through all the chimneys in the 'ouse, and wait on the roof as lookout."

"Thank you, Soot."

"My pleasure, m'lady. I'll come straight down and wake ya as soon as I see him comin'."

"Thank you, Soot," she said again softly. "I don't know what I would do without you."

The ghost doffed his cap. "At yer service, m'lady. Goodnight."

"Goodnight." Stella paused for a moment, before admitting, "I'm scared."

Soot smiled supportively, and rested his hand reassuringly on her shoulder. "Try and feel safe, knowin' that I'm 'ere," he said. Because Soot was a ghost Stella couldn't feel anything when he touched her... except in her heart.

"I will," she replied.

"Now try and sleep, m'lady. I'll be on the roof if ya need me!"

With that the ghost disappeared up the chute, and the cellar was once again plunged into darkness.

Soot expertly made his way up through the house. First he scrambled up the coal chute. Then from the kitchen he made his way to the drawing room with its huge fireplace. That chimney took him up to the first floor. It was as if the house was some giant snakes and ladders board to him.

After a while he had made his way to the very top of
the house. Once there he squeezed himself out of the
chimney pot and on to the roof, which was covered
with a thick layer of snow. Soot was determined to
spot the policeman before the girl's wicked auntie

did. There he sat alone as the blizzard swirled around him.

Soot looked out across the deserted countryside, waiting and waiting all night for a light in the distance.

XX

Absolutely Crackers

It wasn't until dawn that Soot spotted a figure way off in the distance approaching the house on a motorcycle. Snow was still falling from the pale sky, though a little lighter than before. For a moment he wondered if it might be Alberta's motorcycle, but no – there was no sidecar, and it carried a big burly man in a suit and tic, his long brown coat flapping in the wind behind him like a cape. As soon as the ghost saw the figure approach the gates to Saxby Hall, he jumped down the chimney to tell Stella.

"He's here!" exclaimed Soot excitedly, as he raced out of the coal chute and into the cellar.

"Who?"

"The policeman, of course!"

"Thank goodness!" replied the girl, sitting up. "What time is it?"

Being down in the cellar all night in complete darkness was extremely disorientating. Stella had no idea how long she had been asleep.

"It's dawn. Still very early, m'lady."

"Then there's no time to lose. Aunt Alberta is an early riser. We need to get to the front door before the detective rings the bell."

"Then follow me, m'lady," replied Soot, and

together they scrambled up the chute.

The girl's heart was racing as she darted out of the kitchen and down the corridor towards the front door.

Turning the handle she hissed, "I forgot! The front door's locked! And Aunt Alberta's hidden the keys!"

"There must be another way in," replied Soot.

Through the door they could both hear the motorcycle's engine being turned off, and the sound of footsteps trudging through the snow.

"If he rings the doorbell he will wake up Aunt Alberta!" said Stella. She was in an awful panic, but fortunately Soot had an idea.

"Then shout through the letterbox before he does!" replied the ghost.

The girl pushed open the brass flap and called through. "Um, hello!" she said.

The footsteps stopped and a figure crouched in front of the door. All Stella could see was a pair of fierce eyes staring back at her through the letterbox.

"Good morning, miss," said the voice, deep and gruff. "I am Detective Strauss of Scotland Yard." The man flashed up his police badge to the flap. "You are?"

"Lady Stella Saxby," replied the girl.

"Ah yes. My colleague on the telephone told me. I must say you don't look like a Lady!" he scoffed. "More like some kind of... urchin."

"I am so sorry I haven't been able to wash and change, I have been locked in the coal cellar."

"Have you indeed?" His tone was suddenly suspicious.

"Yes, yes I was. I am not lying!" replied the girl, though instantly she regretted saying that as it somehow made it sound like really she was lying. "Thank you so much for coming. I can't tell you how pleased I am that you are here. But now you are here,

I don't quite know where to start." Her mind was racing, and the words were tumbling out. "You see I woke up from a coma and my aunt Alberta told me—"

The detective coughed theatrically. "Ha-hum, do you think it might be better if I take a statement from you face to face, miss?"

"Um, oh yes, of course, Detective Strauss, b-b-but…"

"Yes?" The man was sounding rather weary of all this now.

"I er, don't have the key to the front door."

"You don't have the key?" snorted the detective.

"Yes, I mean no. I mean no I don't have it. I am terribly sorry, sir. I did have it but my aunt's Great Bavarian Mountain Owl snatched it off me."

The detective chuckled to himself and sighed. "With respect, miss, your story is becoming more and more ridiculous by the moment!" His eyes loomed towards the letterbox to meet Stella's. "So it's just another silly little nipper with an overactive imagination. Wasting police time is a serious offence!"

Stella turned to Soot for help. He tried to give his best supportive smile. She didn't dare mention to the detective that she had the ghost of a chimney sweep helping her. If she said that then he would no doubt think she was absolutely **CRACKERS**.

"I am not wasting your time, Mr Strauss," pleaded the girl.

"Detective Strauss, miss!" he corrected.

"Detective Strauss. Sorry."

"Ya can get the garage door open," suggested Soot.

"Oh yes, thank you, Soot," she replied without thinking.

"Who on earth are you talking to, miss?" demanded the Detective.

"N-n-nobody," spluttered Stella. "I mean myself."

"Do you always talk to yourself? It's one of the very first signs of being nuts."

"Um, er, n-n-never!" she replied. "I m-m-mean sometimes. Actually just then. That's the one and only time!"

"If you'll excuse me, miss, I will be on my way!" said the detective curtly, before turning to go.

"No! Don't go! Please!" begged Stella, calling through the letterbox. "Walk around to the garage doors, they are at the end of the house to your left. I can let you into the house there."

"If this is just more of your nonsense I will have no option but to place you under arrest."

"No no, I promise you it's not nonsense!" pleaded the girl.

"It better not be," the detective replied in a very grave tone.

XXI

A Crime Thriller

The detective paced around the wreck of the Rolls Royce. Stella had a good look at him now. Strauss was a portly man, with thick-framed glasses and a shock of wiry black hair. On his upper lip sat a bushy moustache, not unlike a big hairy caterpillar. He very much looked the part of a detective, and could have stepped straight out of a crime thriller. A long brown crumpled mac was worn over an even more crumpled grey suit that seemed at least a size too small for him. His outfit was topped off with that detectives' favourite, a brown felt hat.

Stella watched as the man inspected the damage and made illegible scribbles in his notebook. She caught a glimpse of her reflection in the one window of the Rolls that hadn't been smashed, and hardly recognised herself. She looked awful. It was embarrassing to be seen barefoot and wearing a torn and bedraggled nightdress in front of a total stranger, with black coal dust smeared all over her face and in her hair. No

wonder the detective thought she had the appearance of an urchin. Right now she certainly didn't look like the daughter of a lord and lady, and a lady herself.

As the girl showed the detective the battered car,

Soot had been dispatched to climb down the chimney and into Aunt Alberta's bedroom to make sure she was still sleeping. As soon as Alberta awoke he was to conjure up another of his ghostly disturbances. Anything to keep the wicked woman from seeing the detective. For now. If Stella could convince Strauss that her aunt was responsible for her parents' deaths, there was no reason why he couldn't race upstairs and arrest her on the spot. He could handcuff her while she slept!

The little girl looked on in silence, as the detective lifted the crumpled bonnet of the Rolls Royce and inspected the engine, tapping various parts with his pen. Next he kicked all the tyres with his foot, and knelt down and looked at the undercarriage. Stella wasn't sure what was being achieved by all this, but assumed as Strauss was a detective he must know best. Finally he rose to his feet and announced, "Well, miss, after a thorough inspection of the motor vehicle I can conclude that this was nothing more than a tragic accident. If you will excuse me I will be on my way back to Scotland Yard."

"It wasn't an accident!" pleaded the girl.

"Why ever not?" The detective rolled his eyes.

"Because I believe my papa was poisoned."

This stopped Strauss in his tracks. "Poisoned you say?"

"Y-y-yes," spluttered the girl. Stella was certain of it, but still felt nervous saying it.

The detective pulled his glasses down, and peered over them deep into Stella's eyes. It was clear she had really caught his attention. "Miss, you and I need to sit down so you can tell me absolutely everything you know."

XXII

Shadow of a Doubt

A few moments later the pair were sat opposite each other in the vast library of Saxby Hall. Strauss's legs dangled off the sofa, they were too short for his feet to reach the carpet. Stella tiptoed back over to the door and closed it as gently as she could. She didn't want to wake her aunt, who was still sleeping upstairs.

"What you have to remember, miss," the detective told Stella, "is that there was huge public interest in this case. The lord and lady of a great house losing their lives in a motor-car accident. It was front page of all the newspapers."

Stella hadn't thought about this. It must have been quite a story. "Of course, as with any fatal accident, there followed a thorough police investigation by a team of the very best detectives from Scotland Yard."

"There did?" asked Stella.

"Of course, miss. And after sifting through all the evidence, and interviewing all the witnesses, a team of this country's finest police detectives concluded there were absolutely no signs of foul play."

"They said it was just an accident?" asked Stella. The detective was incredibly compelling, and she was slowly coming round to his way of thinking.

"Yes! Yes they did, miss. Without any shadow of a doubt. Not even a shadow of a shadow of a doubt. Or indeed a shadow of a shadow of a shadow of a doubt. And do you know the one person who came out of this whole sorry story as the hero of the hour?"

"No?"

"Your beautiful aunt Alberta."

The little girl was shocked. Not least at her aunt being described as 'beautiful'.

"She was the first on the scene of the crime, I mean accident."

The girl had no idea. "Really?"

Just then the door of the library slowly opened. Stella jumped up out of her seat. Could it be Aunt Alberta?

As the door swung open it revealed Gibbon. The ancient butler entered the room. He was holding his silver tray. A pair of burning slippers was arranged on it. "Your toasted crumpets, Your Royal Highness!" he announced with a flourish. "Let me just put them down

on the table for you, sir." With that Gibbon dropped
his tray to the floor, sending hot-buttered slippers
flying up into the air. One of the slippers landed
in the detective's lap. It was clearly roasting as he
winced in pain.

"Ow!"

As quickly as he could the detective brushed it off
his lap and on to the floor.

But Gibbon wasn't finished yet. "If you require anything else, sir, just ring this bell," he said, producing an egg timer from the pocket of his dusty frock coat. He balanced the egg timer carefully on the detective's head. "I will be in the library."

Then the butler bowed and left the library, closing the door behind him.

An irritated Strauss took the egg timer off his head, and threw it to the floor.

"Don't mind him, Detective," said the girl. "That's just the butler, Gibbon."

"The man's an imbecile! He should be taken out and flogged!*"

Stella knew Gibbon was by no means the best butler in the world. In fact he might very well be the worst. Still what Strauss had just said was incredibly harsh.

"Now where were we?" continued the detective, clearly irritated by the interruption.

---

*Not sold. Whipped. I know, not nice of the detective at all.

"Erm, you were telling me that my aunt was first on the scene," prompted the girl.

"Oh yes, yes, miss. And the wonderful woman tried desperately to revive your father and mother."

"She did?" The girl was gobsmacked.

"Yes, miss. Sadly there was nothing she could do. They were both killed instantly."

Stella shuddered at the thought.

"Alberta did manage to save you though. She risked her own life pulling you from the wreckage of the burning car."

The little girl took this in. "Sorry," she mumbled. "So sorry, I had absolutely no idea." The detective seemed to know a lot more about what had happened than she did. Of course the accident had sent Stella into a coma, so it was hardly surprising. But now she was beginning to feel guilty about accusing her aunt.

"Miss, you are very lucky to have an aunt like Alberta. Such a kind and caring lady. Beautiful. Talented. The best auntie in the world. Of course you were in hospital at the time of the funeral, but you should know your aunt spoke with great affection in the church. She clearly loved her poor brother and his wife with all her heart. Ms Alberta even sang a wonderful piece of German opera for all the mourners as the two coffins filed out. She has a truly remarkable singing voice."

What?! thought the girl. Stella had had the misfortune of hearing her aunt singing many times over the years. It was like the sound of a cat being throttled.

"She brought every single person in the church to tears," continued the detective.

"Probably because her singing was so terrible!" replied the girl.

"That is a wicked thing to say!" barked the detective. **"HOW DARE YOU?!"**

His anger frightened the little girl and she immediately apologised. "I shouldn't have said that."

"You should be ashamed of yourself, miss," he shouted. **"SHE IS A WORLD-CLASS OPERA SINGER!"**

Stella felt like bursting into tears. This was turning into quite a telling-off.

"Sorry," she mumbled.

"You should be! And whatever you do, don't blub. I cannot abide blubbering nippers. Now where was I...? Oh yes. Two months after the funeral Ms Alberta discharged you herself from the hospital. She knew no one could care for you better than your favourite auntie."

Despite the power of his words, somehow Stella still wasn't entirely convinced by the detective. "Then why did she lock me in the coal cellar?"

Strauss looked ruffled for a moment. "Well, I er, I imagine if she did indeed *place* you there," he was choosing his words very carefully now, "it must have been for your own good. No doubt you were in shock after finding out your parents had been killed in an accident. Shock can lead people to do very strange things. Perhaps, miss, you were trying to run away from home. Am I right?"

There was no doubt that Strauss was a brilliant detective. He seemed to be able to deduce anything. The man knew the answers to questions he hadn't asked yet.

"Y-y-yes," admitted Stella. "I was trying to run away."

"I thought as much. And in this awful weather you could have caught your death of cold. And we can't have that now can we, miss?"

"No," replied the girl.

"Not just yet," murmured the detective under his breath.

"What did you say?" demanded Stella.

"Nothing, miss," replied Strauss innocently.

XXIII

Foul Play

"I am sorry, detective," said Stella as she looked across at him in the library, "but try as I might I can't quite believe it was just an accident. I think it might be…" she hesitated at first, before saying the word, **"murder!"**

"Murder indeed?" Strauss tutted. "And what makes you, young miss, so convinced it was foul play?"

Stella took a deep breath and gathered her thoughts. "Listen, Detective Strauss. My aunt made us all a pot of tea on the morning of the accident."

"What a very kind and caring thing to do," mused the detective.

"Yes! And completely out of character for her!" snapped the girl.

The detective stroked his luxuriant moustache. "I would be very interested in how you can say Aunt Alberta murdered your parents with a pot of tea? Ha ha ha!" The man laughed uproariously at the thought.

The little girl hesitated for a moment before she replied, "Because I think she laced the tea with poison."

The detective fell silent for a moment. He gave the girl a cold, hard stare which sent shivers down her spine. "You think or you know?" he demanded.

"I know. I think. I think I know…" Stella was going to pieces now. It was as if it was she who was being interrogated.

"Miss, I hardly need remind you that it is an extremely grave allegation to make."

Again the girl began to doubt herself. Her version of events started unravelling in her mind like a falling ball of string. However, Stella was sure of one very important thing. "I have read lots of murder mysteries—" she began.

"Oh so this is where all this nonsense is coming from?!" snorted the detective.

"I learned that with most murders the killer has a motive. That's often how the crime is solved. And my aunt had a very strong motive."

"A motive, miss?" chuckled Strauss. "You'll be putting me out of a job! What then could possibly be your aunt's motive?"

The girl took a deep breath before answering, "She wants this whole house all to herself. She always has. Ever since she was a girl."

"Oh, is that so, miss?" The detective's tone was now bitterly sarcastic.

"Yes!" Stella was sure of it. "She keeps on saying I have to sign the deeds to Saxby Hall over to her. Luckily she can't find them anywhere."

Strauss shook his head. "Most likely your aunt just wants to take care of everything for you, miss." The detective had an answer for everything. He hesitated for a moment, before asking Stella, "Of course the deeds would be very useful evidence in this case. You don't happen to know where they are hidden, do you?"

"No." Without thinking the girl's eyes darted over to the shelf of the library where she knew

The Tiddlywinks Rulebook was. Stella couldn't help herself. She was unused to lying, and now was sure she had given away where Papa had hidden the deeds. The girl didn't trust Detective Strauss. If he knew where the deeds were, he may very well give them to Aunt Alberta. Strangely the man seemed to come crashing down on the woman's side on everything.

The detective smiled to himself. "Then why did you look over there to the shelf when you said 'no', miss?"

"I didn't!" protested the girl, unable to stop herself glancing back to the book again.

The detective knew a lie when he heard one. He jumped down from the sofa and waddled over to the bookshelves.

"What are you doing?" asked Stella.

"Just browsing through all the books you have here in Saxby Hall," replied the detective.

"Perhaps I should take you to Papa's study,"

said Stella, gently trying to guide the man out of the
library.

"I don't think so, miss. You run along to the kitchen
and bring me back a glass of your best sherry."

"Now?" gulped Stella.

"Yes. Now!" replied Strauss firmly.

With that he took the girl by her arm and bustled her out of the library, shutting the door behind him with a...

SLAM!

XXIV

Stuffed Owls

Upstairs in Aunt Alberta's bedroom, Soot was crouched in the corner. The ghost had come into the room down the chimney because the woman always kept her bedroom door locked at night. Soot's mission was to keep watch over Alberta as she slept, and tell Stella the moment she stirred. If she woke up and caught her niece talking to a detective, there would be hell to pay.

A huge oil painting of Stella's aunt and Wagner dominated the bedroom in a huge gold frame. On tables and plinths all around her four-poster bed were glass tanks with stuffed owls in them. Owls of every colour and size known to man:

– The miniature Japanese Owl.

– The One-eyed Owl of the Himalayan Mountains or 'Cyclops Owl', thought only to exist in legend.

– The Longbilled Amphibious Owl of Antarctica, which can dive to depths of hundreds of feet in search of fish.

– The Prickly Owl, or
'Owlos Hedgehogius'
to give it its proper
Latin name.

– The half pig/half owl 'Pigowl'.

– The flightless Small-winged Owl of Fiji, 'Owlus
Smallwingius'.

– The Conjoined Twin Owl,
   or 'Two-headed Owl'.

– The featherless Welsh Owl,
'Owlus Baldius'.

– The three-footed 'Tripod Owl'.

– The Furry Arctic Owl, not to be confused with an Arctic roll.*

Hard-of-hearing waiters in restaurants have been known to bring diners an Arctic Owl with a wafer sticking out of it for dessert. Not tasty. Unless you smother it in custard.

It was a deeply sinister sight, even for a ghost, all these magnificent creatures suspended forever in death. The tanks also depicted various woodland scenes, and the birds were all arranged in dramatic poses. One was perched on a branch stretching its wings to fly. Another had a stuffed mouse in its talons. Others were increasingly bizarre:

— **An owl playing the xylophone.**

— **Two owls enjoying a game of badminton.**

— **One in ice skates.**

– Owls fencing.

– Two owls riding a tiny tandem.

– Another in *lederhosen*
performing a traditional
Bavarian beer-festival dance.

– A miniature owl
astride a pony in a
full jockey's outfit.

– An owl dressed as
the World War One
German flying ace,
the Red Baron.

– A pair of owls ballroom dancing.

– An owl breakdancing. This was especially peculiar as breakdancing wasn't invented until the late 1970s.

It would have been clear to anyone who visited Aunt Alberta's bedroom that this woman was completely loopy. In fact not just 'loopy', more 'loopy-loo'. Perhaps even 'loopy-loo-loo'*.

From the far side of the room, Soot could see a figure tucked up under the covers of Alberta's gigantic four-poster bed. Poking out from under the blankets was a head, still sporting the woman's distinctive deer-stalker hat. The sound of snoring was so loud

---

*Or 'loopy-loo-loo-loo.'

it made the furniture shudder.

"ZZZZ*zzzzzzz*...! ZZZZ*zzzz*...!"

After Soot's eyes had roamed around the room they returned to where the figure was sleeping. Just then, he noticed something very strange. Where the woman's foot should have been poking out from under the covers, was a set of talons.

Soot tiptoed over to the bed. Slowly and gently he lifted the blanket, to reveal a huge feathered beast.

It wasn't Aunt Alberta lying there.

It was Wagner!

XXV

Biting the Air

Soot shrieked, waking up the huge bird.

If there is one thing you must know about the Great Bavarian Mountain Owl, it's that the species is not good in the mornings. Oh no. They are by nature nocturnal creatures, so once they go to sleep, they prefer to doze until the afternoon, potter around a bit, have a very late breakfast or brunch, preen their feathers for a while, catch up with the latest owl news, all before they really do anything.

Wake up a Great Bavarian Mountain Owl before noon at your peril.

That's exactly what the unfortunate boy did.

The bird squawked violently at Soot, and hopped up from the bed. He bounced up and down for a short while, trying to peck peck peck at the little ghost. Next the bird flapped his huge wings and took to the air. He chased the boy all around Alberta's bedroom squawking and trying to grab him with his sharp talons. "AAAAAAAAHH!" screamed Soot, as he tried desperately to fend the bird off. He rushed to the door. It was locked.

The owl was pecking at Soot even more ferociously now with his razor-sharp bill.

Like a mouse trapped in a house the boy scuttled around the edges of the room. This was no use, the bird simply dive-bombed him from above. Desperately Soot started trying to hide behind the glass cabinets, but the owl tossed them aside with his powerful wings. Stuffed owls crashed through the glass and on to the floor. It was a macabre sight. Soon Aunt Alberta's bedroom was a mess of broken cabinets, smashed glass and stuffed owls – in strange outfits.

Frantically Soot reached for the nearest object he could find. This happened to be a tiddlywinks set. He lifted it high above his head and crashed it into Wagner's face, sending multicoloured discs flying through the air.

But the great owl kept coming.

Soot had to escape. The only way out was the way he came in. The boy dashed towards the fireplace, and started trying to scrabble up the chimney.

"Aaargh!" he screamed.

The owl had grabbed hold of Soot's foot with his bill and was tugging him back down. With his other foot Soot landed a sharp blow on the bird's head and his bill snapped open to squawk.

"SQUAWK!"

Soot then scrambled up the chimney. With the fireplace well below him he felt safe for a moment. That oversized bird was giving him the screamin' abdabs*! But surely he couldn't follow him up here?

He was wrong.

Soot looked down.

Travelling up the chimney like a missile was Wagner, his eyes gleaming in the dark. The bird's bill was biting the air wildly. He wanted to rip the boy to shreds.

"Noooo...!"

screamed Soot, his cry echoing through all the chimneys and tunnels of the house.

---

*A fright.

XXVI

Lurking Death

Just as Stella was pouring the detective a glass of the finest sherry in the kitchen, he entered the room with a huge grin lurking under his moustache.

The sight of him standing in the doorway when she turned round gave her a fright, and she dropped the sherry decanter.

SMASH!

It joined all the other broken crockery that was strewn across the kitchen floor.

"Stupid girl!" he said.

"Sorry, but you frightened me!" she replied. "I thought you were still in the library."

"No, no, I am all finished in there, miss."

Had Detective Strauss found the deeds? Stella

couldn't be sure.

She had to chose her words carefully now. "So you didn't find anything of interest in there?" she ventured.

"No, miss. Not a sausage."

But was the detective telling the truth? For the moment, Stella had little choice but to believe him.

She looked down at all the broken crockery on the kitchen floor.

"Somewhere down here is the teapot. It's been smashed to pieces, but if I can find just a bit of it you can take it to your laboratory at Scotland Yard and test it for traces of poison." The detective shook his head as the girl sank to her hands and knees, sifting through all the pieces of broken crockery. "It must be here somewhere!"

"I really do not have time for this, miss!" snorted the detective.

"Can you please just help me look for the teapot?"

"No I cannot, miss!" he replied angrily. "This whole investigation is rapidly descending into farce!"

The girl was struggling to find any trace of the teapot. Now she felt foolish that she had allowed Soot to destroy the single best piece of evidence. "If we can't find the teapot, we still might find the poison! Maybe my aunt's hidden it somewhere in here! She might have slipped it out of a tin straight into the teapot!" she exclaimed. Stella rushed to the larder, rifling through the hundreds of jars and tins in there.

Strauss looked on wearily, his impatient sighs making the girl doubt herself and her search seem completely pointless. Soon Stella must have emptied every tin, jar and box in the kitchen, but she couldn't find anything that looked or smelled suspicious. All she unearthed was a mouldy biscuit, the dusty remains of some porridge oats and a small slice of long-forgotten

fruit cake. The slice of cake
now had white mould
growing on the top and
a maggot wriggling
out of it. Much to the
girl's horror the portly
man picked up the slice
and wolfed it down in one.

"I was wondering when you were going to offer
me some cake!" mumbled Strauss, his mouth full.
"So, miss, have you quite finished this ridiculous little
game of yours?"

"No! And it's not a game!" she protested. "You
have to believe me, detective. Aunt Alberta must
have poisoned us all. I am sure of it. Just let me look
through these tins again."

The detective sighed theatrically and made a big
show of looking at his gold pocket watch. "As much
as I would love to see you clear out your kitchen, I
need to be driving back to Scotland Yard before

there is another snowstorm. There is important police business to attend to. Real crimes to solve, real criminals to catch. Not ones drawn from a silly little girl's fanciful imagination."

"B-b-but—!" protested Stella.

"Of course I will need to file a report as soon as I return to Scotland Yard. So I need you to sign this statement I have prepared."

"Statement?" asked Stella.

"Yes, miss, it's standard police procedure, I just need you to sign and date this statement at the bottom here."

The detective dangled an official-looking document in front of her, then twirled it around so quickly it was impossible for her to read.

"What does it say?" Stella's father had always told her never to sign anything she hadn't read through thoroughly first.

"What do you mean 'what does it say'? It is a summary of all your evidence, miss. And acknowledges that you withdraw your allegation because you have realised it is complete and utter nonsense!"

"It's not nonsense!"
"It is nonsense!"
"Not nonsense!"
"Nonsense!"
"Not!"
"Is!"
"NOT!"
"IS!"

If Stella didn't stop this volley of words it would go on until dark. "This is getting very childish, Detective Strauss. Besides, if I am going to even think about signing it, I need to read it first."

The detective's face

began to redden, and he produced a
thick, black ink pen. With every word
he uttered, the man jabbed the
sharp gold nib of the pen towards
the girl. Stella gulped. She was
scared he was going to stab her
with it.

"SIGN. THE.
STATE.
MENT."

"L-l-let me read it
first!"

The detective stopped
and smiled, before trying
another approach. "I will
read it to you, miss, save
you the trouble." With that
the man gathered the piece

of paper so close to his face that Stella couldn't see what was written on it, and proceeded to read aloud.

"Henceforth herewith I, Lady Stella Saxby, do make the following police statement to one Detective Strauss on the date of December the 22nd, 1933 under law ninety-two, paragraph thirty-three, 'B'. My parents Lord and Lady dah-de-dah-de-dum…"

The detective seemed to be skim-reading it now.

"…perished in a motor vehicle crash, la-de-dah-de-dah. I hereby allege was caused by the ingestion of ground-up Lurking-Death Plant seeds in the tea… bum-de-de…um-de-dum…"

The girl fixed the detective with a stare. "What did you just say?"

The man looked up from the piece of paper and stared back at the girl.

"What do you mean, what did I just say?" he demanded.

The girl's eyes widened. "You said something about Lurking-Death Plant seeds being in the tea."

"Did I?" Detective Strauss appeared deeply unsettled.

"Yes! Yes you did!" Stella knew she was on to something. Something big. "And I never mentioned them. Not once!"

"I don't think I did, miss."

"You did! There's no wriggling out of it now!"

At this point the man's face was twitching like mad.

XXVII

Battle of the Billiards Room

As quickly as Soot could scramble further up the chimney, Wagner followed close behind. The owl was snapping wildly at the ghost's heels.

Soot had haunted Saxby Hall for decades, and knew every twist and turn of the house's huge network of chimneys that ran up and down the house behind the walls. As two tunnels met the ghost leaped to one side and tumbled downwards, landing in the fireplace of the billiards room.

This was the place where a long line of Lord Saxbys would entertain their male guests after dinner. Here they would play billiards, smoke the finest cigars and drink whisky from cut-glass tumblers. It had not been used for many years. The huge wooden billiards table still stood proudly in the centre of the room. But its rich green baize top was thick with dust.

Soot tumbled out of the fireplace, crawled across the room and hid behind one of the stout wooden legs of the table.

A moment later Wagner shot out of the chimney, a large cloud of coal dust following him. The great bird flapped his huge wings to disperse it, and settled on the rug for a moment. He glanced around the room then tipped his head down, and inspected the trail of black foot and hand prints that were clearly visible  on the cream rug. They started at the fireplace and stopped somewhere under the billiards table.

The bird had his prey.

Soot stayed as still as he could behind the table leg, desperate not to give himself away. But the owl followed the little patches of coal dust that Soot had left behind, hopping on his talons towards the ghost, slowly and silently.

Finally the bird was on the other side of the table leg. Frozen in fear, Soot could hear the bird breathing.

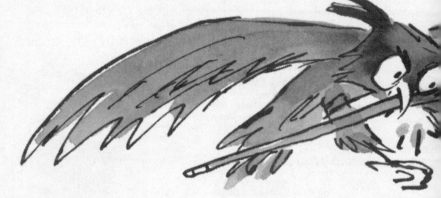

The ghost reached one hand up on to the tabletop, and as silently as he could he grabbed hold of a billiards cue to defend himself. But the wooden cue clunked on the edge of the table, and Wagner hopped to one side.

"SQUAWK!"

The noise the bird made was deafening.

Soot held out the cue in front of him, but before the boy could take a swing at Wagner the owl tore the wooden pole out of his hands with his bill. Then the bird proceeded to snap it clean in two.

SNAP!

However, this gave Soot the chance to leap up out of the way and onto the table. There were a number of coloured balls on the table. Having lived a short life as a chimney sweep Soot had no idea what the different balls were for. But right now he had a good use for them. As the owl hopped up on to the table opposite him, his sharp talons ripping straight through the green baize, Soot picked up one of the white balls. With all his strength he hurled it straight at Wagner. The bird's reflexes were super-sharp. The owl caught the ball between his talons. And Soot could only watch in wonder as the creature proceeded to slowly crush the ball.

CRUNCH.

Wagner turned it to dust.

The ghost leaped off the table and dashed towards the door. The owl rose from the billiards table and zoomed after him. Soot threw any objects he could in the path of the bird. Chairs, books, paintings, even a coffee table. But the bird merely bashed all these things away with his wings, and they crashed against the walls and broke into pieces.

SMASH!

Finally Soot reached the door. Fumbling he just managed to open it. He glanced behind him. The owl was flying towards him at speed. Wagner had stretched his body out long and thin, so he could whiz through the air faster than a bullet.

Soot slammed the door behind him.

SLAM!

A second later there was a colossal

CRASH!

The bird had flown straight into the heavy oak door.

Soot allowed himself a smile as he stood out in the corridor. Keeping his hand on the door handle he was determined to trap the terrifying bird inside.

CRASH!

The door shook at the impact.

The ghost could hardly believe it.

The owl was trying to smash his way out.

CRASH!

Soot could hear the bird's wings flapping again as Wagner took to the air. No doubt circling the billiards room to have one more go.

Soot kept his hand firmly on the handle.

CRASH!

This time the thick wooden door buckled under the impact.

Soot decided to make a run for it. As he fled down the corridor the Great Bavarian Mountain Owl blasted through the door.

BOOM!

Shards of wood exploded everywhere…

SMASH!

...as Wagner landed with a bump on the floor. The owl lay motionless. Had he knocked himself out? The bird was certainly stunned.

The ghost tiptoed along the corridor, and disappeared into the first room he could find, shutting the door silently behind him. It was the nursery. An old rocking horse stood still at the window and a huge railway set was spread out on the floor. There were large books with lots of pictures in them, teddy bears, dolls, toy soldiers, a huge box of marbles, toy cars, even a dog on wheels. It was Soot's favourite room in the house by far. Neither he nor the other children in the workhouse had owned a single toy, so this was a magical place to him.

But as much as he wanted to stay and play, he had to keep moving, and he made his way over to the fireplace and climbed up the chimney.

Back in the darkness of the tunnels he knew he had to find his friend Stella. He had to warn her. Aunt Alberta had not been upstairs in her bed sleeping the whole time after all.

Suddenly it dawned on him exactly where she was. In an instant he knew the girl was in terrible danger.

XXVIII

Under the Cover of Darkness

Now would you like to know what Aunt Alberta was growing in her greenhouse?

I thought you might.

This greenhouse sat at the end of the long sloping lawn of Saxby Hall. Alberta had blacked out the windows by painting all the panes of glass, and put a huge metal padlock on the door. It was strictly out of bounds to Stella, as it was to everyone else in the family. Absolutely no one was allowed in there, not even Wagner. Once a young Stella asked her aunt how these plants could thrive without sunlight. She was told that "these particular plants only grow in the dark." This only served to make the girl even more intrigued as to what was inside, but Alberta guarded her greenhouse jealously, and Stella could never even sneak a peek.

Of course Alberta had been growing the Lurking-Death Plant there for ten years, waiting for the right time to put its poisonous seeds to use. It was just one of many rare plants that Alberta had been growing under the cover of darkness for decades. They were secret plants, which very few people in the world knew about. They were all so deadly that Alberta had to tend to them in her thick leather gloves.

These are just some of the plants Alberta grew in her greenhouse:

– The Black Rose.
Beautiful to look at, but if you pricked your finger on a thorn – beware. They contained a venom so strong it could kill an elephant.

– Fatal Fruit. These purple dangling fruits would take a bite out of you before you could take a bite out of them.

– The Bush of Doom. Legend has it that the bush's branches could strangle a grown man to death.

– Voodoodoo Ferns. These plants could be burned in ancient magic rituals to commit evil.

– Witch's Moss. A noxious smelling moss that could lead to severe choking and even death.

– Whispering Lilies. These
were known to whisper
bad things about you when
your back was turned, and
slowly send you mad.

– Creeping Conifers. Known to
move around in the dark, before
they pounced.

– Hypnotic Hydrangeas. These could make you lose
weight or stop smoking, but were equally likely to
hypnotise you into committing terrible crimes.

– Cruelberry. Their sweet
smell made many people
believe that cruelberries
were safe to eat. One tiny
bite would kill you instantly.

– Hissing Orchid. When
you bent down to sniff it, it
would squirt poison at you.

Let's return to the story. Right now in the kitchen
Detective Strauss was breaking into a terrible sweat.

The man had mentioned the Lurking-Death Plant
as part of Stella's proposed police statement. How
on earth had he known about that? Stella had only
supposed her parents had been poisoned, she didn't
know how exactly. It was all coming together in the
girl's mind now. The ground-up seeds of the Lurking-
Death Plant must have been what Alberta had put in

the family's tea that fateful morning. That was why Stella blacked out. That was why the Rolls Royce crashed. Poor Mama and Papa hadn't stood a chance.

Now Detective Strauss had given himself away. He knew more than he was letting on. Much, much more.

Anxiously the man jabbed the pen towards the girl. "Just sign the statement at the bottom here, miss."

"No!" Stella was growing in confidence now. "How did you know that my aunt grew strange plants in her greenhouse?!"

Stella had turned the tables on the detective. Now she was interrogating him!

"You are becoming delusional, miss! I never said anything about a Lurking-Death Plant!"

"Yes you did!" insisted Stella.

At this moment the detective was sweating like mad, and his luxuriant moustache seemed to be starting to… peel off. The moisture had evidently dislodged the glue and now the moustache was hanging off his upper lip.

"Your moustache is coming off!" exclaimed the girl.

"Don't be absurd, miss! I grew it only this morning!" With that the man turned his back to her and rearranged whatever it was he had stuck on his upper lip. When he turned back around Stella saw he had managed to put the thing back on upside down.

"It's the wrong way up!" shouted the girl.

As the man fiddled frantically with his fake facial hair, Stella snatched the piece of paper from out of his hand. Her eyes scanned it as quickly as they could. It wasn't a police report at all. It was the deeds to Saxby Hall! The very deeds that her awful aunt needed her niece to sign so that the house could finally be hers.

"It's you! Isn't it?!" exclaimed the girl.

"Very well yes, child, it is me," the wicked woman purred, ripping off her thick-framed glasses, which formed part of her disguise. "Your beloved Aunt Alberta."

XXIX

Grisly Toupee

"He's Aunt Alberta!" exclaimed Soot, as he landed with a bump in the fireplace of the kitchen, a black cloud of coal dust following him.

"Yes!" replied Stella without thinking. "I know! Her moustache just fell off."

Aunt Alberta's sharp black eyes scanned the room. "Who are you talking to, child?" she demanded. "Tell me! WHO?!"

Stella followed her aunt's gaze. The woman was looking straight past where the ghost was standing.

"Nobody!" snapped the girl. Stella was desperate for her secret weapon to remain a secret.

"What do you mean 'nobody'?" Aunt Alberta was becoming more suspicious by the second. "You looked right over there and spoke." She pushed the girl down on to a chair, before marching over to the fireplace and looking up the chimney. Soot edged to one side, with his mouth now firmly shut.

"Hello?" called Alberta up the tunnel.

The word echoed up and down. *Hello Helloo Hellooo*. Hearing the echo she couldn't resist actually shouting, "Echo."

It too echoed up and down.

Echo echo echo...

"There's no one up there!" said the girl.

"Then who were you speaking to?!" demanded Aunt Alberta.

Stella had to think fast. "I was just talking to my imaginary friend!"

The woman marched back over to her. "*My imaginary friend*," she repeated, mocking her young niece's tone. "What a big baby you are!" It seemed like Aunt Alberta had fallen for it. "I haven't had an imaginary friend myself for at least five years now! What's his name?"

Stella said the first thing that came into her head. "King Kong."

It was the name of a film she had seen that year at the pictures with her papa. She had no idea why she chose that.

"What does this King Kong do?" asked Alberta.

"He's a giant monkey." Stella knew it sounded stupid but by this time it was too late.

Imaginary friends can of course come in all shapes and sizes. There are many strange ones children sometimes choose:

**A PRINCESS
FROM TUDOR
TIMES**

A MARTIAN

A PIXIE

A LEPRECHAUN

**A TALKING
TEDDY BEAR**

**THE MONSTER
WHO LIVES
UNDER YOUR
BED**

A FRIENDLY DRAGON

A MEDIEVAL KNIGHT

A CAVE BOY

A KANGAROO

A VENTRILOQUIST DUMMY

KING KONG

Alberta scoffed at the thought that her niece had chosen King Kong of all things to be her imaginary friend. "You are talking to a giant monkey! You really should know better by now. How old are you, child?"

"I'll be thirteen on Christmas Eve."

"Oh yes. Of course you will. That's in just two days' time," Alberta reflected. "Anyway, is this the same imaginary friend you were talking to in the garage last night?" her aunt went on.

"Y-y-you heard me in the garage?" Stella felt sick to her stomach that she had been spied on and not had the faintest idea.

"Oh yes!" exclaimed the woman, a sinister smile snaking across her face. "I heard every word."

Alberta took her pipe out of her pocket, and lit it. Slowly she took a few puffs of that sickly sweet smelling tobacco. It was clear the woman wanted to savour this moment, a moment where she could expound on her genius. Then, as the sound of flapping wings hummed down the corridor, Alberta looked away from her niece for a moment. Behind her back, Stella mouthed 'HIDE' to Soot. The ghost nodded, and just before the giant bird flew through the doorway to the kitchen, he was safely back up the chimney.

"Ah, good morning, my darling," Aunt Alberta said, as the owl came to rest on her arm. She gave Wagner a lingering kiss on his bill. The bird fluttered his wings and bobbed his head. Turning back to Stella, Alberta began again, "Last night I was out in the garden putting the finishing touches to my snow-owl."

"Snow-owl?" asked Stella.

"Yes," continued the woman. "Surely you have heard of a snow-owl, child? It's like a snowman, but a little more, how can I say…"

"Owly?" ventured the girl.

"Exactly!"

Stella had spotted the huge icy figure on the

lawn, but she had no idea it was meant to be an owl. There seemed no end to her aunt's obsession with the large-headed species of bird.

"Then I saw a light in the window of the garage. I thought that was strange. When I approached the doors, I heard your voice. Somehow you had escaped from the cellar. Are you going to tell me how?"

The girl had to think fast. She didn't want her aunt to know she had used the chute. Then she might block it off and all the chimneys.

"I er, um, I found a spare key to the door on the floor of the coal cellar!"

Aunt Alberta's eyes narrowed. "Did you really?"

"Y-y-yes. So I tiptoed upstairs and went to look at what had happened to the Rolls. I thought you were probably asleep so I didn't want to wake you."

"Mmm..." murmured the woman. "A likely story! Then I heard you talking about the tea being poisoned. I needed to find out exactly how much you really knew. I leaned on the doors so I could listen in closer. I must have leaned too hard because they burst open."

"I remember!" exclaimed the girl. It was all coming together in her mind now – why Alberta had set up this elaborate plan of disguising herself as a detective.

"Yes, child, you very nearly saw me. But when you closed the doors again I kept listening in. Then you said you were going to call the police. Naughty niece! Your auntie didn't like that. Oh no, your auntie didn't like that at all." The woman tutted playfully and smiled. "That's when I started to hatch this ingenious plan of mine."

"So you cut the telephone line?" asked Stella. "I knew there was no dialling tone!"

"Exactly right. Then I picked up the telephone in my room and pretended to be the operator, then the police. This suit I am wearing I found tucked right at the back of your father's wardrobe. He won't be needing it any more! Ha ha!"

"You are despicable!"

"I know! And I chose the name 'Strauss'* as he is my second-favourite German composer. The moustache was a trimmed owl feather, coloured in with ink and stuck on with some glue. As for the wig,

---

*Johann Strauss is the famous German composer of "The Blue Danube". Not to be confused with Johanna Strauss, who never composed a note of music, but did make terrific fudge.

I skinned a rat I was saving to feed Wagner, trimmed it with scissors to fit, and then pinned it onto my head." Alberta then whipped the thing off, revealing her shock of red hair underneath. Stella was horrified at the sight of this grisly toupee; especially on realising the rat's tail was still attached. "Then all I had to do was disconnect my motorcycle from the sidecar and I had you completely fooled! Clever, aren't I?"

Aunt Alberta looked exceptionally pleased with herself. She was, in a word, smug.

"No!" replied Stella.

The woman's eyes narrowed. "What do you mean 'No'?"

"You're not *that* clever Auntie. You gave yourself away. You let it slip that you ground up seeds from one of *your* deadly plants in your greenhouse and added them to our tea the morning of the crash!"

"It was the perfect plan. Poison everyone and then blame it all on an automobile accident," said Aunt Alberta lightly, before the tone of her voice darkened. "But then I thought you had gone and ruined it by surviving."

"I knew the tea tasted funny!" exclaimed the girl. "I poured mine out into a pot plant."

"I wondered why my begonia had died," murmured Alberta. "Anyway, when your father's will was read out I realised I needed you alive, long enough for me to get you to sign over the deeds anyway. I can't believe my idiot brother wrote that if you died Saxby Hall should be sold and all the money given to the poor. Who cares about those grubby little peasants?"

The girl fixed the woman with a stare. "What you have to remember, Auntie, is that you can never win!"

"Is that so?" purred Alberta.

"Yes, because I will never sign those deeds over! Never ever ever!" announced Stella. "Do what you want to me, but Saxby Hall will never be yours!"

Alberta smirked. It was as if the whole thing was a game to her. "Then, child, let me introduce you to... the Owl-Rack!"

XXX

The Owl-Rack

The Owl-Rack was a piece of equipment designed especially by Aunt Alberta herself. The woman had built it just before she entered Wagner into the Owl Annual Fair, or OAF for short. It was a beauty pageant for owls as CRUFTS is for dogs.

There were numerous competition categories:

* Softest plumage
* Shiniest bill
* Twistiest neck
* Tallest owl
* Longest wingspan
* Loudest twit-wooing
* Largest owlet egg
* Bushiest eyebrows

* Scratchiest claws

* Aerial skills

* The most rodents gobbled down in one minute

* Sweetest-smelling owl droppings

Alberta being Alberta, she wanted to come first in every category. Of course that included the prize for 'Tallest owl'. Just like with her tiddlywinks, if she had to cheat to win, so be it. From subscribing to *Owl & Owling Magazine* she had learned of a famous owl breeder in Sweden, Oddmund Oddmund, who owned a Norwegian Owl named Magnus. He fed it a ton of pickled herring a day and it had grown to well over four feet tall.

Even on his tipclaws Wagner was actually only 3ft 11 inches, so didn't have a chance of winning this particular category.

So deep in Alberta's dark mind she dreamed up the Owl-Rack. Next she secretly went about building it. It was a devilishly simple device.

There was a three-step system for making your owl taller:

1) You strap the owl to the Owl-Rack by its wings and feet.

2) You turn the handle.

3) You turn the handle again.

Wagner squawked the house down when he was first tied to it. The pain of being stretched was intense. Winning an OAF gold medal for 'Tallest owl' wasn't as important to him as it was to his mistress, but he had little choice in the matter.

As it happened Wagner's rival owl in the height stakes, Magnus, was so obese from eating a ton of pickled herring a day, his owner Oddmund Oddmund had to roll him into the exhibition hall. Under strict OAF rules the owl was instantly disqualified, as all owls had to fly into the exhibition hall. Oddmund Oddmund appealed the decision to the judges, and attempted to demonstrate that Magnus could indeed

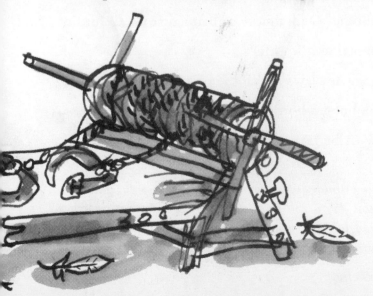

fly by firing his obese owl out of a cannon. However, Magnus crash-landed on the judge's table, and ended up crushing three of them to death. From that moment on Oddmund Oddmund was banned from all future owl competitions for life.*

Wagner flew away with the prize for 'Tallest owl', and took home a horde of other owl statuettes[+] too.

Now Alberta was going to use the Owl-Rack

---

*Oddmund Oddmund began breeding penguins instead, and to this day is the world-record holder for owning the fattest penguin who ever lived – Agneta, who weighed 6 tonnes, around the same as an African elephant.

[+]Or 'owluettes'.

as an instrument of torture on her own niece. If this terrible contraption didn't make her sign over the deeds to Saxby Hall, nothing would. The device was kept in a tiny attic room at the very top of the house, bare of all furniture except an empty old wardrobe. It was a room Stella didn't even know existed.

Up in the attic Alberta tied Stella to the rack. As much as the girl tried to kick her legs or pull her arms, once strapped to the machine she couldn't move. Perched on the window ledge throughout was Wagner, shifting uneasily from foot to foot on seeing the rack again. Behind him, Stella could see the blizzard once more raging outside the window.

Aunt Alberta's face contorted into one of twisted glee as she turned the handle on her contraption, pulling the girl's skinny legs and arms in opposite directions. **"Aaaaaarrrrgggg ghhhh!!!"** screamed the girl.

"Sign the paper!" demanded Alberta.

"Never!" replied Stella through the pain.

"Sign it!" Her aunt twisted the handle again.

"Aaaaaarrrrgggg ghhhh!!!"

Wagner covered his eyes with his wings. Perhaps it was seeing the little girl in pain, perhaps it was the fact that it was bringing back memories of being on the rack himself, but the owl couldn't bear to watch.

"Well then, child, I am going to have to leave you tied to the rack, with no food or water. And every time I come back I will turn the handle tighter. Tighter and tighter and tighter until your arms and legs will be yanked clean off."

It was a terrifying image. Stella was rather attached to her arms and legs. But she was determined not to show any fear.

"You will give in the end, child," uttered Aunt Alberta.

"No! No! I won't! Never!" Stella exclaimed.

"Oh yes you will," replied her aunt. "Whether it will be tonight, or tomorrow, or the next day, or the day after, or the day after that, you will break in the end. Soon you will be begging me to let you sign over the deeds to the house. Then Saxby Hall will finally be mine! All mine!"

"You are a monster!" shouted the girl.

Aunt Alberta took this as a compliment. "Oh thank you. A monster? I am not sure I have ever been called that before. Such high praise! Now before I go, I'll have one last itsy-bitsy little turn."

This time Alberta spun the handle with all her strength. Stella's arms and legs were nearly yanked out of their sockets.

"AAAAAAAARRRRRRRGGG GGGHHHHHHHHHHHHH!!!!!!!!"

she screamed. The girl had never known pain like it. Her whole body convulsed in agony. It was as if she had been struck by lightning.

"Toodle-pip!" said Alberta with a giggle. "Wagner!"

With that the owl flew to his mistress's arm, and the pair left the room. The girl listened as the door was locked behind her, followed by the sound of footsteps going down the stairs.

"Soot!" she hissed.

The boy appeared from up the chimney, looking very upset. "I am so sorry m'lady, I wanted to help, but I had to keep meself 'idden."

"You did the right thing, Soot. Now get me out

of this thing."

Soot rushed over to the Owl-Rack and started turning the handle.

"AAARGH!" Stella screamed. "Other way!"

"Sorry!" said Soot. He quickly turned the handle in the other direction, releasing the strain on the girl's poor arms and legs. Fumbling he untied Stella's hands and feet from the leather straps. Faltering a little, she stood up.

"I must say ya do look taller, m'lady," observed the ghost.

"Oh well, that's fine then!" replied Stella sarcastically.

"So wot's the plan now, m'lady?"

Stella thought for a moment, before a smile lit up her tear-stained face. "We start the fight back!"

XXXI

Ants in Pants

Stella's thinking was simple. The girl now had to fight to force this evil woman out of her home. Forever. Alberta had killed her mother and father. Now she would stop at nothing to force Stella to sign over Saxby Hall to her, even resorting to torture.

Together in the attic, she and Soot began dreaming up the most diabolical tricks they could play on Alberta. They needed tricks that were sure to make the girl's aunt scurry away from Saxby Hall screaming for mercy!

Stella found it hard to think of anything at first. She'd had such a sheltered upbringing, growing up in a vast country house and educated at a posh school for girls.

"Let's hide one of each of her pairs of socks! Then when she puts them on in the morning they will be odd!" she exclaimed.

Soot pulled a face. The boy had never even owned a pair of socks, so the idea of torturing Alberta by making her wear odd ones sounded lame.

"With respect, m'lady. That is a load of tosh!"

Stella was more than a little offended. "Well, I would like to hear your suggestions!"

Soot thought for a moment. Having grown up in a workhouse he had learned you had to be tough just to survive. He had seen the boys play the meanest tricks on each other in the years he spent there. "We need to put ants in her pants!"

"Ants in her pants?" asked the girl.

"Yep. And that's just for starters!"

For a moment Stella looked shocked, but then her face lit up at the thought. Soon she was trying to top Soot's idea.

"Flood her floor with marbles!"

The ghost went further still. "Make 'er pipe go boom!"

In just a few minutes together they had a long list of tricks:

- Put a nest of ants from the garden in her knicker drawer.

- Flood her carpet with marbles. There was a huge box of them in the nursery.

- Take all the tobacco out of her pipe and substitute it with gunpowder from a shotgun cartridge found in the drawer of Papa's desk in his study.

- Mix the bubbliest bubble bath from Mama's bathroom in with the woman's toothpaste.

- Cut open her bar of soap and put black boot polish from the kitchen inside.

- Go to the garage to find a shard of glass from the Rolls Royce's cracked windscreen. Then place it in her toilet bowl so when she pees it sprays right back up at her!

The pair was so enthused dreaming up the list, they could have added to it until dawn. However, there was no time to lose, and they immediately set to work putting their plans into action. As they could hear Aunt Alberta snoring downstairs in her bedroom they knew they were safe for a little while at least.

The tiny fireplace in the attic would be their escape route. It was quite a squeeze, but once inside they could use all of Saxby Hall's vast network of chimneys and chutes. Together they would have the full run of the house. So Stella followed Soot into the attic chimney, just managing to squeeze her body inside.

All through the night they climbed up and down the
vast network of tunnels and chutes, gathering all the
props they needed to play tricks on the nasty auntie.

Just as the two were spreading marbles on to the carpet in Alberta's room as she slept, her beloved owl tucked up in bed next to her, Stella noticed something.

The curtains were beginning to glow with the sun behind them – dawn was breaking. The pair quickly disappeared into the fireplace in Alberta's bedroom, and climbed back up to the attic. Once there Soot tied Stella back to the Owl-Rack so Aunt Alberta would be fooled into thinking her niece hadn't moved all night.

Downstairs, the grandfather clock chimed six o'clock, waking Aunt Alberta up.

BONG BONG BONG BONG BONG BONG.

The fun was about to begin!

XXXII

"My Bottom! My Bottom!"

Aunt Alberta sat up in bed. She gave Wagner, who was wearing matching striped pyjamas, a poke. It was time for her to give the Owl-Rack another almighty turn and get back to the important business of torturing her niece.

First Alberta went to stand up. But instead of her feet touching the carpet as they did every morning, she placed them on a sea of marbles. The little glass balls rolled under her weight, and with a giant

WHOOSH!

Alberta flew into the air and landed on her behind with a

CRASH!

"OW!" she screamed. The woman picked up a handful of marbles. "How the blazes did these get here?!"

Again and again Alberta tried to stand up, but every time she did she fell back down again. The hundreds of little glass balls made her roll every which way. So, on her hands and knees, she crawled to her bathroom, and pulled herself on to the toilet. Immediately there was a feeling of immense relief. This lasted less than a second though, as she felt her wee-wee spurting back up at her! Her behind soaking wet, and with her pyjama bottoms still round her ankles, she jumped up from the toilet shouting,

"Nooooo!!!"

After taking a deep breath to gather herself, Alberta peered down into the toilet bowl. Try as she might she couldn't see anything amiss. The piece of glass the pair had put there had been perfectly positioned on top of the water so as not to arouse the slightest suspicion. So she sat down and tried again.

"Nooooooooooo!!!!" she screamed,

as her wee-wee came back to haunt her once more.

Still desperately needing to pee, but abandoning the toilet for now, the woman moved over to the sink to have a wash instead. She ran the taps, and wetted her bar of soap under the water. Next Alberta closed her eyes and rubbed the soap on to her face, giving herself what she thought was a jolly good wash. However, a shock was awaiting her. When she opened her eyes and looked in the mirror she saw what she thought was a stranger looking back at her.

In fact it was her own face, but painted completely black.

"NNNNNNNNNNNNO OOOOOOOOOOOOOOO!!!!"

she cried in horror.

Try as she might to wash it off by using more of the soap it just became worse and worse. Now her hands and neck were completely black too. Alberta put the tip of the soap into her mouth to taste it.

"Eurgh! It's boot polish!"

In the mirror she inspected her now-black tongue. Desperate to brush it clean she reached for her toothbrush and toothpaste. Alberta squeezed what she assumed was nothing more than her favourite minty-fresh toothpaste on to her brush. Now of course she was becoming suspicious. Just as she was about to put it in her mouth she sniffed it. The paste smelled minty so she began to brush away at her black tongue.

But as soon as she began brushing, the bubble bath Soot and Stella had mixed in with the paste began to foam. Huge soapy bubbles started foaming out of her mouth. The more furiously she brushed the bigger the bubbles and soon the bathroom was filled with them. "There is devilment at work here!" she hollered.

Upstairs in the attic, Stella and Soot listened to each new yelp from the woman. Every one made them laugh more and more.

Back in her bedroom, Alberta threw a blanket over the marbles so she could walk to her chest of drawers. Determined to get to the bottom of this, she rushed to get dressed. First she slipped on a pair of her massive knickers, as big as a child's tent. As soon as she had them on she noticed a peculiar tingling sensation. The tingling became worse and worse, until it felt like her bottom was on fire.

"My bottom! MY BOTTOM!" she howled, as she began leaping up and down and moving wildly around the bedroom. It was if she was doing some ludicrous new dance routine all of her own invention. Wagner was now sat up in bed, and watching the display. The owl had seen his mistress do some bizarre things in his time, but this was off the scale.

The ants in her pants were working like magic.

The woman jerked and juddered her way over to her armchair, and reached for her pipe. Her tobacco never failed to make everything seem better for her. Aunt Alberta placed the pipe to her mouth before guiding a lit match to the tobacco chamber.

Except there wasn't any tobacco in there.

It was gunpowder.

KAB

XXXIII

A Game of Cat and Mouse

It would be something of an understatement to say the woman wasn't happy. Aunt Alberta was FURIOUS. With boot polish on her face, bubbles foaming at her mouth, her red hair singed from the explosion and ants wriggling around her knickers, she charged upstairs to the attic.

Alberta knew her niece must somehow be responsible.

She burst through the door in an attempt to capture the girl red-handed. However, much to her surprise, Stella was exactly as Alberta had left her, fastened to the Owl-Rack.

On seeing her aunt's startling appearance, half-dressed, jerking around wildly, the girl couldn't help but giggle.

"Oh this is funny, is it?!" asked Alberta, not expecting an answer.

"No, it's not," replied the girl. "More HILARIOUS!" With that Stella hooted with uncontrollable laughter.

"HA HA HA!"

"Well maybe you will find this hilarious!" said the woman, as she twisted the handle on the rack again and again and again.

"AAAaaaaaaaarrrrrrrgg GGGGGHHHHHHH!" the girl screamed.

"I don't see you laughing now!"

"No," said the girl through the pain. "But it is still funny!"

A fuming Alberta turned the handle again, and Stella's arms and legs were yanked apart.

Sadly the tricks hadn't worked. Alberta hadn't fled from Saxby Hall screaming. Instead she was now on the warpath. "I know all those tricks were you, but how did you do it, child? I tied you to the rack myself, and the door was locked from the outside. There was no escape."

"I don't know what you are talking about," protested the girl.

"You know *exactly* what I am talking about," purred Aunt Alberta. She leaned over her niece's face, and looked deep into her eyes. "I know you are lying."

The woman paced around the attic, looking for clues. First she peered out of the tiny window, to see if anyone was dangling from the snowy ledge by their fingertips. Next she tiptoed over to the huge oak cupboard that stood in the corner of the room. In the blink of an eye she pulled open the door and was bitterly disappointed not to find anyone hiding inside. Alberta stole a glance back at her niece. Without thinking Stella looked over to the fireplace. No! She had given herself away again. This was where Soot was standing, observing this game of cat and mouse.

"So," hissed the woman, "I was right. There is a clue in the chimney."

"I don't know what you mean," uttered the girl.

"You are a very bad liar, child."

"No I am not!" protested Stella, before suddenly becoming mightily confused as to whether it was good to deny being a bad liar. That meant you were a good liar.

"Yesterday you looked over to the fireplace in the kitchen," continued Alberta. "There's a clue to all this up there. I know it!"

The woman slunk over to the fireplace. Invisible to her, Soot stepped out of the way. As she got down on her hands and knees to look up the chimney, the ghost came up with a plan.

Soot rushed over to the cupboard. He squeezed behind it and with all his strength started pushing it towards Aunt Alberta. As the wooden feet of the wardrobe squeaked on the floorboards, the woman looked up. But it was too late. Soot toppled the cupboard over her, and with a huge thump as it hit the floor, it trapped her inside.

"Let me out! Let me out of here at once!" came an enraged voice from inside.

"Top work, Soot!" exclaimed the girl.

"Thank ya, m'lady!"

"Now get me out of this thing!"

As the cupboard twitched on the floor with Aunt Alberta flailing around beneath it, the ghost untied Stella's hands and feet from the Owl-Rack.

"Wagner! WAGNER!"

bellowed the woman, as the pair fled down the stairs. Just as they reached the next stairwell they ducked, and the giant owl skimmed their heads on his way up to the attic.

As they reached the landing Stella nearly ran slap-bang into Gibbon. The butler was shaking hands with a pot plant and saying, "Do come and stay again, Major."

"So where now, m'lady?" asked Soot.

"The garage," replied the girl. "I have an idea."

XXXIV

The Driving Lesson

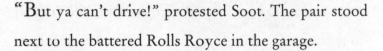

"But ya can't drive!" protested Soot. The pair stood next to the battered Rolls Royce in the garage.

"Not really, no," conceded Stella. "But it's my only chance of escape. I can't stay here a moment longer, or she'll have me back on that Owl-Rack until my arms and legs are ripped off!"

"I know, m'lady, but…"

"No buts! Look, if I can get up enough speed I can smash through the gates and be at the nearest village in no time."

"It's too dangerous!" The ghost was not convinced. The last thing he wanted was for his friend to kill herself trying to escape.

"I've seen my father drive this thing tons of times.

How hard can it be?"

Stella was a very headstrong little girl, and she pulled open the door of the smashed-up family Rolls, and jumped in.

"Use ya mincers! Ya feet don't even reach the pedals!" observed the ghost.

"Er, what on earth are mincers?" Stella exclaimed.

"Mincers – mince pies – eyes, a course." Soot shrugged.

Stella shook her head despairingly, then looked down at her feet, which were dangling off the enormous black-leather driving seat.

"What do you need the pedals for?" she asked innocently.

"Oh give me strength!" he exclaimed. "Only a girl would say that!"

Stella did not appreciate this comment at all. "You

are a chimney sweep! How are you the expert on driving? I bet you've never even been in a motor car. And certainly not a Rolls Royce!"

This was true. Only very rich people owned motor cars at the time Soot was alive. And only incredibly rich people owned a Rolls Royce.

"No I ain't! But I know how they work."

"Oh really! And how is that?" Stella was losing her patience with him.

"I am a boy," he reasoned. "All boys just know about these fings."

This infuriated Stella. As a girl she knew for a fact that girls were infinitely better at everything than boys. "Oh do they?!" Her tone was deeply sarcastic. There was no way she was going to let Soot have all the fun of driving the car just because he was a stupid boy. "Well then, if you know everything about the motor car, you can give me my first driving lesson!"

The ghost was not at all convinced that this was a good idea. "But m'lady—" he protested.

"There isn't time to discuss this any more! Now get in!"

Soot did what he was told and climbed into the Rolls Royce.

"And you can work the pedals too!" ordered the girl. "Whatever they might be for."

The ghost installed himself in the footwell, just under the girl's dangling feet.

"Right, so how much do ya know?" asked Soot.

"Well, I know I have got to hold this big round thing."

"The steering wheel! Yes! Yer going to get us both killed."

"With respect, Soot, you are already dead."

"I stand corrected, m'lady," sighed Soot. "First fing ya need to do is turn the key in the ignition."

The girl did so, and with Soot pressing down on the accelerator pedal with his hand, the engine roared.

"It still goes!" exclaimed Stella. "I knew the old Rolls wouldn't let me down."

"Now ya see that long thin fing to yer left?" asked Soot.

Stella rested her hand on it. "Yes."

"That's the gear stick. When I say, move it forward and to the left."

While keeping one hand on the accelerator, Soot moved his other to the clutch pedal. **"NOW!"** he shouted.

The car started lurching forwards.

"Soot?"

"Wot?"

"We forgot to open the garage doors."

"Hold tight!" exclaimed Soot. The ghost pushed down as hard as he could on the accelerator pedal and the engine roared. The Rolls Royce sped forward…

SMASH!

It burst through the huge garage doors. Shards of wood flew everywhere, as the Rolls skidded out onto the icy drive. The cold winter air blasted through the broken windscreen, making the girl's eyes water. The old motor car had been very badly damaged by the crash, the front wheels were buckled, and one of the back tyres had burst. So the car would be incredibly

difficult to control even for a racing driver. Nonetheless they continued steadily along the drive, heading for the gates – and freedom. As the engine growled Soot shouted, "Change gear!"

Stella fumbled with the stick, and suddenly the car lurched to a halt and started travelling backwards towards the house at enormous speed.

"That's reverse!" yelled the ghost, before stamping his hand on the brake, and the car spun round and round on the spot before juddering to a stop.

"First gear again. Up left."

The girl carefully followed his instruction.

"Now second gear, sharp down left."

Now the Rolls was chugging along at a good pace. There was so much snow everywhere it was very difficult to tell where the drive ended and the lawn began. She just managed to swerve around some trees, and avoid a head-on collision with the huge snow-owl Aunt Alberta had been building. Then the tall iron gates at the end of the drive were coming into view.

"The gates are getting closer," Stella called down excitedly.

Just then they heard the deafening roar of a motorcycle engine. It was Aunt Alberta, racing towards them with Wagner installed in the sidecar.

Both Alberta and her owl were sporting matching leather flying helmets and goggles.

"It's my aunt!" exclaimed Stella. "She's right behind us!"

Soot slammed his hand down on the accelerator.

"Hold tight!" said the ghost. "We have to go as fast as we can to get through those gates."

Stella looked over her shoulder. "They're gaining on us!" she cried.

"Straight to fourth gear then. Down right!" hollered Soot over the din of the engine.

There was an almighty crunching sound as the girl yanked the stick and the gears shifted. Safely now in fourth gear the Rolls was going faster and faster. The huge iron gates were seconds away from impact.

"Any moment NOW!" shouted Stella, and she closed her eyes as the Rolls rammed the gates...

CRASH!

...and came to a juddering halt.

"Cor blimey!"

"Yes, now we are for it!" said Stella with a gulp.

XXXV

The Frozen Lake

The back end of the Rolls Royce was thrown high up into the air with the force of the impact, before coming down with a colossal thud. The car sat still on the icy drive. It would take a tank to smash through the huge iron gates to Saxby Hall.

A short distance behind them, Alberta brought her motorcycle skidding to a stop. The woman lifted up her goggles and smiled gleefully as she surveyed the scene.

"Are ya all right, m'lady?" asked Soot, looking up from the footwell of the Rolls Royce.

Stella was still sat in the driving seat. But she had hit her head on the steering wheel and now all she could see was stars. "Yes. I am just dazed that's all."

Astride her motorcycle, Alberta looked devilishly pleased with herself. "It looks like the end of the road for you, young lady," she called out. "Now, I think it's time you came back inside, and finally signed the deeds to Saxby Hall over to me. There's a good girl."

Stella whispered to Soot, "We can't give up now. There must be another way out. Has the Rolls got any power left?"

"There's only one way to find out," he replied. "Throw it into reverse."

The girl did so and the motor car wobbled backwards. The collision had crumpled the entire front section of the Rolls even more than before. The grille stayed lodged on the gates, but the engine was still coughing and spluttering away.

Alberta's smile turned to a scowl as she realised that her niece still had some fight left in her.

"First!" shouted Soot. Stella changed gear, and the Rolls rattled off, with Alberta in hot pursuit.

VRoooooooom!

The Rolls sped across the vast grounds of Saxby Hall, with the motorcycle not far behind. The thick covering of snow was now being thrown up in the air by the spinning wheels of both motor vehicles. Stella tried twisting the steering wheel from side to side, in an effort to spray snow into Aunt Alberta's path. However, this did very little to stop the evil woman from gaining on them. Alberta's motorcycle had special snow-spikes fitted to the tyres, which kept it dead on course.

"STOP HER!" ordered Aunt Alberta. Wagner clambered out of the sidecar and on to his mistress's shoulders. For a moment they looked like a motorcycle display team, before Wagner launched himself into flight.

The Great Bavarian Mountain Owl can reach speeds of up to one hundred miles an hour. Wagner shot off high into the sky. As the motor car sped on,

Stella looked up out of her **window** to see where the owl had gone. Then Wagner **landed** with a thud on to the bonnet of the Rolls, **his huge** feet denting the metal. The owl looked straight at Stella, his wide chest completely blocking her view.

"I can't see where we're going!" shouted the girl.

"Hold tight! I'll put the brake on!" replied Soot.

But they were going too fast, and instead of stopping the car started spinning and spinning around.

Wagner wobbled and launched himself back into the air. Now Stella could see the car was spinning uncontrollably towards the frozen lake at the end of the lawn.

"Brake!"

she screamed.

Soot had both hands on the pedal, pushing down as hard as he could. "I am braking!" he cried.

Time seemed to both slow down and speed up as the battered Rolls Royce spun out on to the ice. As it reached the middle of the lake, the motor car finally stopped gliding, and the engine cut out with a final splutter. Desperately Stella tried to restart the car, but the trusty Rolls Royce was finally dead.

Alberta stopped her motorcycle at the bank, and switched her engine off. Wagner flew back on to her leather glove. The silence was like thunder. For a moment it was incredibly peaceful. Then came the sound of a crack.

CRACK,

Quiet at first, then becoming louder and louder and multiplying into the sound of thousands of cracks.

CRACK CRACK CRACK CRACK CRACK CRACK CRACK CRACK CRACK CRACK,

Stella looked out of the window. The huge sheet of
unbroken ice covering the lake below them was now
an elaborate pattern of interconnecting lines. The
heavy motor car jolted to the side, as the section of
ice it was resting on started to break up under its
titanic weight.

"Help!" screamed the girl, as the icy water began to flood the car.

Soot climbed up from the footwell. "Yer in grave danger, m'lady," he cried. "You 'ave to save yerself."

But as the icy water rose from her feet to her ankles to her knees to her waist Stella became frozen with fear. As much as she wanted to she couldn't move, and soon her eyes glazed over and all she could see in her mind's eye was her body floating beneath the ice.

"M'lady!" shouted the ghost. "Climb on to the roof!"

Shivering uncontrollably with the cold, Stella just managed to pull herself out of the car and on to its roof. Still barefoot, she started slipping and sliding, very nearly toppling into the icy waters below. She could see her aunt laughing to herself from the safety of the bank.

"I am frightened, Soot. I don't want to die," said the girl.

"Nah, I wouldn't recommend it," replied the ghost.

"And what about you?" she asked.

"Don't worry about me, m'lady. Ya have to save yerself."

"So, child. I win again! Are you finally ready to sign those pesky deedy-weedies?" bellowed the evil woman, her deep voice soaring over the ice.

The battered Rolls Royce was sinking at an alarming rate, and now was just a few inches away from being completely submerged. The ice surrounding the car was broken into tiny pieces, there was no way Stella could run across it to safety. If she tried to dive in and swim, the water was so cold she would die within moments.

"Ya have to do wot she says," said Soot. The ghost was going under fast with the car, and within seconds only his head, leaning out of the Rolls window,

was above the surface of the water. As the cold water rose up his body, his ghostly form almost seemed to evaporate into the water. "It's yer only 'ope!"

Stella, still balanced on the car's sinking roof, was up to her knees in icy water.

"Well, Stella?" bellowed Alberta. "What's it to be?"

"I'll sign the deeds!" Stella shouted back.

"Now that wasn't too hardy-wardy, was it?" mused her aunt. "Wagner! Bring her to me!"

The giant bird took off from her hand once more and swooped over the ice. Just as Stella was up to her chest in the frozen lake, the owl's talons lifted her upwards by her shoulders. Soon they were flying through the freezing morning air.

"Be careful, m'lady!" called the ghost. The girl looked back as Soot and the once-beautiful Rolls disappeared into the lake, until his little ghostly cap floating on the water was all that she could see of him.

"Nooooo!" cried the girl.

Wagner dropped the tearful girl on the lake shore at his mistress's feet. Freezing, dishevelled and broken, Stella lay on the ground. There was no point fighting any more. She didn't have the strength. Aunt Alberta had won. The wicked woman looked down at this wretched creature, shivering in her soggy nightdress, her face stinging with tears, and chuckled to herself cruelly.

"I knew you would come round to my way of thinking in the endy-wendy."

XXXVI

Easy-peasy-poo

Now Aunt Alberta had her niece exactly where she wanted, she couldn't have been nicer. In the drawing room of Saxby Hall, she wrapped the girl in a big warm blanket, and sat her on the comfiest sofa in front of the fire.

"There we are, young lady," said the woman, as she handed Stella a large cup of piping-hot soup. "We must warm you up for the little issue of the signing of those pesky deedy-weedies."

In her heart the girl knew that she should never ever sign over the deeds of Saxby Hall to her wicked aunt. But her heart was broken. Stella's body and spirit had been crushed by the past days and nights of terror. With her parents gone, and Soot trapped at the bottom of the icy lake, she felt she had nothing left to live for. If she signed now perhaps this nightmare would be over.

"Let me just get you a penny-wenny," said the woman brightly.

Stella stared into the fire and sipped her soup.

Aunt Alberta returned with the document and a quill made from a huge owl feather, and sat next to her niece on the sofa.

"You don't need to go to all the trouble of reading it! Good gracious no! It's all terribly tedious!" she chuckled. "Just put your signature at the bottom-wottomy there, there's a good girly-wirly."

Stella reached out for the quill. Her hand was still shaking so much from the cold that she couldn't hold it properly.

"Dearest child, let your aunty-waunty give you a helping handy-wandy-pandy." With that the woman wrapped her niece's hand in hers and slowly brought the quill to the paper. "Let me make this easy-peasy-poo for you," she added. With one hand she held the girl's shaking hand still, and with the other she moved the piece of paper around until Stella's signature was at the bottom of the deeds.

Saxby Hall was now finally hers.

Aunt Alberta wept with joy. It was the first time Stella had seen the woman show such emotion. She skipped around the drawing room, and rushed over to Wagner, who was sitting on his perch, to give him a big sloppy kiss on his bill. Then she began dancing and singing a little made-up song about herself.

"All hail me, Lady Saxby…" After the first line the song ground to a halt, however, as it was clear Alberta couldn't think of anything to rhyme with Saxby'.*

"Do you know what I am going to do with this place, child?"

"No, Aunt Alberta, I don't," replied the girl, before continuing in a sarcastic tone, "but I'm sure you are going to tell me."

"You're right. I am," continued the woman. "First thing tomorrow I am going to burn the whole thing down!"

---

*To be fair to the woman, it is quite hard.

XXXVII

Burn Burn Burn

Sitting opposite her aunt in the vast drawing room, Stella couldn't believe what she was hearing. Saxby Hall had been in her family for centuries. "Burn it down? You can't!"

"Oh yes I can!" replied Alberta. "I can do whatever I like with it, child. It's mine now. It's going to burn burn burn! And as soon as it's a pile of ash I am going to start building the world's largest owl museum."

Stella thought for a moment, before she asked, "Are there any others?"

"No, that's why it will be the largest!"

Stella couldn't quite follow her aunt's logic, but now there was no stopping the woman. From a nearby shelf she pulled out a huge rolled-up sheet of plans, and presented them proudly to her niece. "I have been working on this for years. Lady Alberta's Owleum."

The plans showed a vast owl-shaped concrete building, with various different rooms. These included:

– An owl cinema. This was for the showing of owl-related films only, though none had actually been made yet.

– An owl café, selling treats made purely from owl-droppings, e.g. owl-dropping flapjacks, owl-dropping pâté on owl-dropping toast, owl-dropping chocolate truffles (an ideal gift for an elderly relative you might want to get rid of).

– A huge library, containing all the books written about owls over the years. All seven of them.

– An owl grooming salon.

– Three types of toilet, Gentlemen, Ladies and Owls.

– A lecture hall, where Aunt Alberta could make four-hour-long speeches about the history of owls.

– A gift shop, selling owl bookmarks, thimbles, stationery sets, porcelain figurines, key rings and lawnmowers. Plus a huge selection of gramophone records of twit-wooing.

– An owl-free room. This was a room designed for those visitors with zero interest in owls. It would have an owl in it.

"My Owleum will make me a fortune!" proclaimed the woman, just getting into her flow now. "Millions of fellow owl enthusiasts will come from all over the world…"

Millions? thought Stella. The girl was pretty sure it was only Aunt Alberta who was a fully paid-up member of the Official Owl Fan-Club.

"The visitors will enter here," said the woman, pointing at the entrance. "Where they will be welcomed by a solid gold statue of myself."

"You are completely crackers."

"You're too kind! Praise praise praise!" replied the lady with a smile. "Once through here you will be able to feast your eyes on every single species of owl from around the world. Stuffed."

"Stuffed?" asked the girl. Wagner's ears pricked up at this word.

"Yes, child. Stuffed. Owls are much better behaved when they are stuffed. Then in the centre of the Owleum, in a huge glass case, will be my beloved Wagner."

The bird started squawking now, and jolting around violently on his perch.

"The largest Great Bavarian Mountain Owl ever seen in captivity. Stuffed under glass for all eternity."

Stella couldn't help but notice how violently the bird was reacting to Alberta's plans, almost as if he understood every word she was saying, so she pushed her aunt further. "So I imagine you are going to wait for Wagner to die of natural causes?"

"Oh no!" replied the woman. "He'll be all old and grey then. No. I will shoot him first thing tomorrow. Stuff him in his prime!"

Wagner was now frantically circling the room at speed squawking like crazy. As Alberta returned her attention to the plans for her Owleum, Stella thought all this might be enough of a distraction to slip away unnoticed. She started tiptoeing out of the drawing room.

Just as she had reached the door, Alberta barked, "And where do you think you are going?"

"I, er, um," Stella was becoming very jumpy now, but tried to make what she was saying sound as casual as possible. "Well, I, er, was just going to pop upstairs, quick bath, maybe finally get changed out of this nightdress, and think about making a move."

"You're not going anywhere, child," replied

Aunt Alberta, her voice suddenly taking on a deeply menacing tone.

The girl looked into her aunt's black eyes. "N-no?" she stammered.

"Oh no. You know far too much. I have been arranging another little 'accident'. Especially-wecially for you."

"An a-a-accident?"

"Yes!" Aunt Alberta smirked. "And this one you definitely won't survive!"

XXXVIII

The Perfect Murder

The evil auntie had masterminded an elaborate end for her young niece. "You can't get away with this!" cried Stella.

"Oh yes I can, child," replied Aunt Alberta softly. "It's the perfect murder, because the murder weapon will simply melt away."

"Melt away?" Stella was baffled. "What on earth do you mean?"

"Come with me and I will show you."

The woman grabbed the girl by the hand, and led her out of the drawing room and on to the long sloping snow-coated lawn. At the end of it, casting a huge shadow, stood Aunt Alberta's sculpture in ice. **"My snow-owl!"** declaimed the woman proudly. "It's finally finished. Beautiful, isn't it?"

"Why are you sh-sh-showing me this?" asked the girl, shivering from the cold once more.

"Because in a few moments, this snow-owl is going to topple over and crush you to death. I will call the police immediately to report you missing. But they won't find you until the spring, when the murder weapon will have simply melted away. Quite brilliant, aren't I?"

"S-s-sick more like!" replied the girl, struggling as hard as she could to escape the woman's strong grasp.

Alberta looked down at her niece and smiled a sinister smile.

"Go on then child, run for your life." She let go of the girl, who fell to her knees. Now Stella was crawling through the snow, desperate to get to her feet to make a run for it. But the snow was deep, and she was cold and tired and didn't have any strength left.

Aunt Alberta rushed around to the other side of the snow-owl, and rested her shoulder against it. With

all her might she began to push. Just then Wagner
dive-bombed his mistress from high in the sky. The
giant owl clawed at her, trying to make her stop. Stella
realised she had been right, he must have understood
when Alberta said she wanted him stuffed.

"Wagner! WAGNER! What is the meaning of this!" screamed Alberta.

But the bird kept on trying to pull her away, so the large lady punched Wagner as hard as she could right on the bill.

This sent the poor owl spiralling to the ground unconscious.

The wicked woman went back to pushing as hard as she could at her snow sculpture. Slowly but surely the huge figure began to topple over towards her niece.

"Goodbye, Stella!" she called out. The girl looked up. A huge mass of snow and ice was falling towards her. In an instant it was going to crush her to death.

"Noooo!"

cried the girl.

SMASH!

Just then Stella felt herself being knocked high up into the air!

WHOOSH!

Gibbon had crashed slap-bang into her. The ancient butler had travelled down the long sloping lawn at speed standing on his silver tray, much like he had accidentally invented snowboarding.

In one hand he held a hot-water bottle, in the other two champagne flutes. "The finest Dom Perignon, sir!" he announced.

Without knowing it the butler had saved the young girl's life. Quite by accident Gibbon had knocked her clear of the falling snow-owl. Stella landed on the lawn with a…

THUD!

"Thank you, Gibbon," said Stella, more than a little dazed as she sat up in the snow.

But the ancient butler merely shook himself down, completely oblivious as normal. "It's frightfully hot in here, sir. Before I go, should I open a window?"

XXXIX

The Big Bad Wolf

Aunt Alberta was now lying face down in her snow-owl, having fallen on top of it. As she slowly rose to her feet, her face went a furious red. She started wading across the lawn and through the deep snow towards her niece. Her anger had given her a powerful energy. Even though the snow was up to her knees, Alberta's pace was quickening all the time.

The little girl dashed towards the Hall's front door. Her aunt had left it ajar. Just as Stella had bolted it shut from the inside Alberta started thumping on the door.
BANG
        BANG BANG!
The door shuddered with the force of her heavy hands.

Alberta pushed open the letterbox and called through it, "Little pig, little pig, let me come in!"

The girl took a step back from the door. "No! Never!"

"Then I'll huff, and I'll puff… and I'll smash the door in!"

There was an eerie silence for a moment, before Alberta returned with a huge snow shovel. The woman huffed and puffed, as the spade crashed through the heavy door…

CRASH!

... sending splinters of wood flying.

Stella took another step backwards. It was only a matter of seconds before Aunt Alberta was going to completely demolish the door. The girl had to think fast. The fireplace! Alberta was far too fat to fit up there. So Stella made a run for the nearest one, situated in the dining room.

As Stella raced along the corridor she heard the front door slam off its hinges and crash to the floor.

CRASH!

Alberta stepped inside the house.

"Come to the big bad wolf!" shouted Alberta, wielding the shovel above her head like a weapon.

The girl darted into the dining room, and dashed over to the fireplace. Just as she was disappearing up the tunnel…

SNATCH!

Alberta grabbed her by her ankles. Stella looked down to see her aunt lying at the bottom of the chimney staring up at her. As the girl struggled, she dislodged a mass of soot that had been stuck up the flue. It dropped down on to Alberta, filling her eyes and mouth with the thick black dust.

"AAAARRRRRGGGHHH!"

she cried.

As the evil woman choked she couldn't help letting go the grip on her niece. As soon as her legs were free, the girl hurried up the chimney. Soon she was out of reach of her awful auntie.

"You can't escape," snapped Alberta. "I know just how to deal with nasty little children who climb up chimneys. I've done it before and it works an absolute treat. I am going to light a fire!"

XL

The End of a Mystery

"What do you mean you've done it before?" called down Stella from the chimney. The girl couldn't believe what she was hearing. That was exactly how Soot had told her he had been killed.

"You might as well know it was me who made my baby brother, your uncle Herbert, disappear all those years ago," said Aunt Alberta from the fireplace of the dining room.

"Of course!" said Stella, almost to herself. What happened to the baby had remained a mystery for over three decades.

"When he was born I knew he would inherit Saxby Hall, and not me," explained Aunt Alberta. "I hated him for it! Much as I hated your father. So in the dead

of night I crept into his nursery and smuggled him out of the house."

"How could you do such a thing?" demanded the girl.

"Remarkably easily," replied Alberta. "I took him down to the river, put him in a wooden box and set him afloat. I thought the river would swallow him up. But ten years later, there he was on the doorstep of Saxby Hall dressed as a—"

"CHIMNEY SWEEP!" exclaimed Stella. Soot – she had to mean Soot!

"That's right." Alberta was completely taken aback that the little girl had said this. "How on earth did you know that?"

"Because the ghost of a chimney sweep haunted this house."

"Ghosts aren't real, you stupid little child!"

"Yes they are! That's who has been helping me."

"You are completely delusional!" After everything, still the woman refused to believe. Soot had been right – grown-ups' minds were too closed to believe in anything other than the here and now.

As much as Stella wanted to continue her escape, she was intrigued to know the full story. "How did you know the chimney sweep was your baby brother?"

"Because he was the image of my other brother Chester, your father. Shorter and skinnier all right, the little urchin had grown up in a workhouse living on scraps of food – but he was the absolute spit of Chester. And this revolting stinking little urchin kept on saying he felt like he had been to Saxby Hall before.

It was only a matter of time until the rest of the family worked out who he was too. So I waited until he had crawled up the chimney to clean it, and then I lit the fire below."

"You are a monster!"

"The best part of it was I let one of the servants take the blame."

Soot is really my uncle! thought the girl. This was explosive news. "That boy is the rightful heir to Saxby Hall!" she exclaimed.

"He was a child. He died many years ago now. Just another little chimney sweep that no one mourned."

Stella thought for a moment. "My mother, my father, my uncle… How many more people are you going to murder?"

"Just one," replied Aunt Alberta. "You!"

XLI

Hide-and-Seek

The woman set to work in the dining room, striking a match and lighting the fire. Soon plumes of thick black smoke were snaking up the chimney. Desperately Stella started clambering upwards again. Her eyes were watering buckets. In next to no time she could hardly breathe.

Within moments the smoke had plunged the shaft into total darkness. Now she couldn't see a thing. Suddenly Stella lost her grip and was falling down the tunnel straight towards the fire. Her body bounced off the sides of the chimney, sending soot raining down alongside her. So much soot fell that it put out the fire. **"DARN IT!"** shouted Alberta, as Stella managed to halt her fall just inches above the open fireplace and begin to clamber her way back up. Soon she had reached the very top of the house, and squeezed herself out of the chimney pot and on to the roof. Stella lay there for a moment on the snow, gasping to fill her lungs with air.

But just as the girl opened her eyes, she saw the top of a ladder appear at the edge of the roof. There was no stopping this evil woman! Soon a shock of soot-encrusted red hair appeared, then two sharp black eyes, then a wicked grin.

"Our little game of hide-and-seek is over! Auntie's found you!"

The woman hoisted herself up on to the roof, and stood for a moment, wobbling slightly. "Now it's your choice, child. Would you prefer to jump? Or shall I give you a nice little pushy-wushy?"

By this time it was night, and Alberta's silhouette was framed by a full moon, hanging low in the winter sky.

"You'll never get away with this!" shouted the girl, clinging in terror to the chimney pot.

"Oh yes I will. I have got away with everything so far. If you are very lucky I may even sing at your funeral!"

"I'd rather you didn't!" replied Stella. "When you sing you sound like a foghorn!"

"How dare you!" Aunt Alberta lurched towards her, but lost her footing on the snow.

BUMP!

She slid down the roof on her bulging belly.

"AAAAARRRRGGGGHHHHH!!!!"

Just as Stella was hoping the woman might plunge to her death, she managed to grab on to the guttering with her fingers. At first there was silence as Alberta dangled there, then the girl heard her aunt say, "Stella? Erm, Stella-wella?" Her voice was soft and sweet now, as if she was the nicest auntie in the world.

"**What?!**" demanded the girl.

"Would you mind awfully giving your dear old auntie a handy-wandy?"

"**No!**"

"Pleasey-weasy?"

"Why on earth should I?" demanded the girl.

Alberta's weight was too much for her short, stubby fingers. One by one they were beginning to slip off the guttering.

The tone of her voice darkened. "Child, if you don't help me, you're going to get the blame for everything. Your parents' little 'accident'. Killing your dear old auntie."

"But I never did!" protested Stella.

"That's not how it's going to look. Oh no." Alberta's words were slithering around the girl's mind now like a snake. "The whole country will see you as a cold-hearted killer. You'll be locked away for a hundred years. That's if they don't send you straight to the hangman!"

Stella didn't know what to think anymore. "B-b-but I haven't done anything wrong!" she protested.

"Letting me die like this would be murder. **M,U,D,D,E,R!**"

This wasn't the time to correct her aunt's spelling, so the girl kept silent.

"Your dear mama and papa brought you up to be a nice young lady, didn't they?

"Y-y-yes…"

"You don't want them to be ashamed of their only child, do you?"

"N-n-no…"

"Then give me your hand," said Alberta. "I promise I won't hurt you."

Tentatively Stella slid herself on her bottom down the sloping roof towards her aunt.

"There's a good girl," encouraged her aunt. "Trust me, child. I promise nothing bad is going to happen."

Stella stretched out her hand towards the woman. Alberta grabbed it firmly, and yanked her niece off the roof.

"Aaaaaah!" screamed the girl as she flew through the air. She just managed to grab on to Alberta's ankle.

The woman looked down at the girl, clinging on

for dear life.

"If I can't have Saxby Hall, then no one can!"

With that the woman let go of the guttering, and the pair plunged down...

"Arrghhh!"

XLII

Dead Calm

Suddenly there was the sound of two huge wings flapping. An owl shot through the night air.

WHOOSH!

Stella could feel herself being grabbed as Wagner snatched her from her fall.

Aunt Alberta hit the snow below with a gigantic…

THUD!

Wagner set the girl down gently before hopping over to his mistress. Stella followed close behind. They needed to check if this evil woman was really dead.

Alberta's body had fallen on to a large pile of cleared snow. It lay there perfectly still. There wasn't even the sound of a gurgle or the slightest twitch. All was silent.

Dead calm.

Stella breathed a sigh of relief. Then, just as she was about to turn away, she saw the woman's little finger move. Then her hand. Then her arm. Dazed and confused, Alberta pushed herself up to her feet. The snow stayed stuck to her. She looked like the Abominable Snowman.*

Alberta stood there, wobbling for a moment, before she wiped her eyes clear of snow. She hadn't been injured at all. The huge pile of snow had broken her fall.

A great big white furry ape that lives in the Himalayan Mountains in Nepal.

"Now, where were we?" said Alberta with a smile. "Oh yes. I was just about to bump you off!"

As the girl made a run for it across the lawn, Wagner shot off into the sky. As he circled in the air, he started squawking wildly.

"SQUAWK SQUAWK SQUAWK!"

It was a sound the girl had never heard the owl make before.

Not far off in the trees surrounding Saxby Hall, a chorus of hoots could suddenly be heard. The birds were calling back to Wagner. The branches of the trees rustled as hundreds of owls took to the sky.

For Stella there was no time to think about what was happening. She had to run. But where to? The girl stumbled in the snow. Her aunt caught up with her, and pulled a flail from her inside pocket, and swung it around her head.

WHOOP WHOOP WHOOP

Alberta must have snatched it from the suit of armour in the hall. The flail was a particularly nasty weapon. It had a long wooden handle, with a chain at the top, and a deadly spiked metal ball at the end. It could kill a man with one strike. This particular flail hadn't been used as a weapon for hundreds of years. Until now.

"Please, Alberta. I am begging you..." pleaded Stella.

WHOOP WHOOP WHOOP:

Still the woman swung the flail faster and faster around her head.

"I hope your pathetic little life is flashing before your eyes child! Because this is the end. **E, N, E, D.** END!"

With that Alberta swung the flail up in the air.

"Nooooo!"

screamed Stella.

But before she could rain it down on Stella... hundreds of owls whooshed down from above.

ZOOM!

From the tiniest owlet to the largest great grey owl, together they seized the woman in their claws and with one motion carried her off into the sky.

"Aaaaaaaaaaaaarrrrrrr rgggggggghhhhhhhh!!!!!!!!" she cried as the flail dropped out of her hand and fell on to the snowy lawn. THUD!

From the roof Wagner was squawking loudly, no doubt calling out orders to his fellow owls.

All Stella could do was watch in amazement. Aunt Alberta kicked and screamed as the squadron of owls carried her off, high into the night sky. The snow fell off her as they took her up up up, way above the clouds. Soon the large lady was little more than a tiny dot. Stella didn't dare blink. She needed to know that this really was the end of the story.

"SQUAWK!" Wagner called out a deafeningly loud command to his feathered friends up in the air.

At once they all let go of the wicked woman with their claws.

"AAAAAAAAAAAAAA ARGGGGGGHHHHH!"

screamed Alberta as she tumbled down down down through the sky.

From far off in a distant field there was a deafening **THUD!** as her body hit the ground. Stella wobbled as the earth shook a little.

At last her awful auntie was no more. The little girl sighed with relief, before calling the brave owl over. "Wagner!" The bird hopped back to where the girl was standing. "Thank you," she said, and wrapped her arms around him. Slowly but surely he lengthened his wings, and wrapped them around her too.

"You saved my life," whispered the girl.

The great bird twit-wooed softly in reply. Stella didn't know what the owl meant exactly, but somehow she understood. "Wagner, I still need your help." The bird tilted his head to one side. He was listening. The girl used gestures to help explain herself better. "I need you to fly me over the lake." Stella pointed to it. "We need to find Soot... I mean my uncle."

The girl climbed on to the bird's back, and held tight to the feather tufts on the top of his head. With the added weight Wagner needed a run up so he could take

off, but take off he did. To Stella this was thrilling, it felt like she was piloting an aeroplane. It was the most splendid sensation. Flying. The stars above her, the wind in her hair. As the owl glided high over the lake, she looked down to see if there was any sign of the ghost. The floating shards of ice glistened under the light of the moon. Now it all looked so calm and still, with little trace of the drama that had unfolded on the ice earlier that day.

First Stella spotted the shadowy shape of the Rolls Royce, which had sunk into the depths below. Then the girl caught a glimpse of a tiny figure far under the ice at the bottom of the lake, wrapped in frozen reeds.

"There!" she pointed. Wagner followed her hand down, and they landed on the largest piece of ice they could find.

"He's at the bottom!" said Stella, peering over the edge of the ice into the freezing depths below. The girl wasn't sure if a ghost could die again. But as she watched him lying motionless with no expression on his face, she feared the worst. Then she heard a

SPLASH!

as Wagner dived in. Stella watched in amazement as the brave owl swam down to fetch the boy. Wagner bit onto Soot's shirt with his bill, and powered back up to the surface.

The girl knelt down and hauled the ghost on to the ice, before helping the owl up too. Wagner shook himself dry, as Stella bent over the poor lifeless figure.

"Uncle Herbert..." she whispered. "Uncle Herbert."

The ghost spat some water out, which hit the girl right on the nose. "Who on earth is Uncle 'Erbert?" he asked.

"You're alive!" she exclaimed.

"Nah, I'm dead," came the reply. The ghost looked at the girl as if she was daft.

"Oh yes," replied Stella.

"And who's this Uncle 'Erbert?"

"It's you! In fact to give you your full title, Lord Herbert Saxby of Saxby Hall!"

"Leave it out!" The ghost shook his head. "Have ya been at the sherry, m'lady?"

XLIII

Promise

Once safely back inside Saxby Hall, the pair sat together in the drawing room. The girl rekindled the fire, and told Soot the whole story. How Alberta was really his sister, and had put him in a box and floated him down river when he was a baby.

"That's how the people at the workhouse said I had been found!" Soot exclaimed. "Floating down the River Thames in a box."

Stella told her uncle how his wicked sister had recognised him on his return, and had deliberately lit the fire to be rid of him forever.

Soot was amazed, but it was all coming together in his mind. "That day I showed up at Saxby Hall, I knew I'd been here before. I could feel in it in me bones."

The ghost's eyes widened as he took all of this in. "Well, who'd have thunked it. Little ol' me! A lord! Ha ha!" The chimney sweep laughed uproariously at the idea, and began affecting what he thought sounded like a posh accent. "'Ello, I am a lord, don't ya know? Wot wot!"

Now Stella was laughing too. "But it's true! This whole place is rightfully yours! I feel bad now for thinking you were just some little oik."

Soot chuckled. "No need, m'lady."

"I shouldn't have been such a snob. Now I know it really doesn't matter if you grew up in a workhouse or a palace. We are all the same really."

The ghost smiled at her. "We certainly are, m'lady."

"You don't have to keep calling me that. Just Stella will be fine."

"Right ya are, m'lady Stella."

The pair chuckled together, then Soot couldn't resist saying with a cheeky smile, "But ya have to call me yer lordship!"

Just then the great grandfather clock in the hallway chimed midnight.

BONG BONG BONG BONG BONG BONG BONG BONG BONG BONG BONG BONG.

It was Christmas Eve, Stella realised. Her birthday.

"I've just turned thirteen!" she said excitedly.

The ghost looked crestfallen at the thought.

"What's the matter?" she asked.

"Yer growing up. Very soon ya won't be able

to see me any more."

"I'll always be able to see you!" Stella protested.

"No." The ghost shook his head. "Grown-ups never can."

It was hard for Stella to notice at first, but the outline of the ghost was becoming fainter.

"You *are* fading…" she said softly.

"What did I tell ya, m'lady? We best say goodbye now."

"But I don't want you to go," she pleaded. "You're all the family I've got left."

"I am not goin' anywhere," replied the ghost.

"But you are vanishing now! Right in front of my eyes."

"I told ya I would! Ya wanted nuffink more than to be older, but bein' a child is such a special fing. When yer a child, ya can see all the magic in the world."

The girl's heart was breaking. "Then I don't ever want to be a grown-up!"

The ghost's light was almost gone now. Stella didn't dare blink in case when she opened her eyes he would be gone altogether.

"Everyone has to grow up in the end," replied the ghost. "But even though ya won't be able to see me, I'll always be 'ere, right at yer side. Now promise me one fing, m'lady."

The ghost was becoming fainter and fainter now.

"Yes! Yes! What?" pleaded Stella.

"Promise me that even though ya can't see the magic in the world with yer eyes any more, you'll believe in it in yer 'eart."

"I promise," she whispered.

The last thing Stella could make out was the faintest outline of the ghost's smile.

And then he was gone.

Epilogue

It was an unusual Christmas Day lunch that year at Saxby Hall. Just the three of them sat around the long dining table. Stella, Wagner and Gibbon. Instead of the traditional turkey with all the trimmings, the ancient butler served up a roast hedge. It was very tough, and not at all tasty, but it was the thought that counted.

As Boxing Day came and went the girl realised she needed to face the truth of what was to now become of her. As much as she wanted to stay at Saxby Hall, Stella knew she couldn't look after the whole house on her own. So she reconnected the telephone, and called for help.

Being still legally a child, those in charge decided that Stella needed to be packed off to an orphanage. Only when she reached the age of eighteen could she officially inherit Saxby Hall. The orphanage was teeming with children who had also lost their parents, or had never known them. It was home to the poorest of the poor.

Despite the best efforts of the kindly matron who ran it, the orphanage was incredibly cramped. The hundreds of children shared one dormitory. They had to sleep four to a bed. Baths were just once a month. There was nowhere they could go to play outside.

Of course Stella had grown up in a life of privilege, in a vast country house. Though she did her best to hide it, living at the orphanage made her sad. Now Stella understood why poor Soot had run away from the workhouse. Some nights she would cry herself to sleep. Stella wished for life to be better not just for her, but for all the children there.

So one morning she went to the matron with an idea. Why not move the whole orphanage to Saxby Hall?

"If you are sure, Lady Saxby," said the matron.

"It's just Stella, and yes I am sure," replied the girl. "What use is a huge house like that with no people inside?"

A big smile spread across the matron's face. "It's

a splendid idea! The children will absolutely love it!"

Indeed they did. At last all the little ones had their own beds. There were piping-hot baths every night. In summer there were games on the lawn, and swimming in the lake.

In fact it always felt like summer at Saxby Hall now. The ancient butler Gibbon kept all the orphans entertained with his antics. Some of the braver children even went for rides on the back of a Great Bavarian Mountain Owl called Wagner.

Of course Stella grew up, but Saxby Hall stayed a home for children. It was the happiest orphanage in the world.

SAXBY HALL
A HOME FOR
ALL CHILDREN

Today if you visit there, you might see a very old woman out on the lawn playing games with some of the young orphans.

That very old woman's name is Stella. Stella Saxby. She is over ninety years old and doesn't let anyone call her 'Lady' any more. Just 'Stella' is fine.

If you are a child, you might just be able to make out something else.

Something none of the grown-ups can see.

The ghost of a little chimney sweep, playing happily with all the other children on the lawn.

A LETTER OF COMPLAINT

Dear Reader,

Let me introduce myself. My name is Raj and I run a newsagent's shop. I am well known for my excellent special offers. Just today I am selling 17 bottles of lemonade for the price of 18. So far I have had a starring role in all six of David Walliams's (yes that really is his name) books. 'The Boy in the Sari' was the first, followed by 'Mr Smell', 'Millionaire Man', 'Granny the Gangster', 'Ratnugget', and finally 'Demon Dental Hygienist'.

Now imagine my surprise when I read his latest

effort 'Naughty Auntie' to find that I, Raj, have been completely left out. Personally I thought the book was very boring as it was all set in the olden days. Who cares? Rubbish! I much prefer Ronald Dahl.

Being completely left out of this book made me furious. So furious in fact that I crushed a piece of fudge with my bare hands. I know, very manly.

Most children who come into my shop tell me they only read Mr Willybums' (or whatever his stupid name is) books because I, Raj, have a starring role in them. There is a growing army of Raj fans, or 'Raj-o-philes' as they have become known. Like me they skim through all the tedious bits to find the chapters I am in.

Therefore, I am asking you to join me in signing the petition over the page stating that I, Raj, will be reinstated in his next book. I have also written to the Prime Minister and the Queen, both of whom wrote me very nice letters back requesting I do not ever contact them again.

If Mr Winklebottoms (he might as well be called that) has any sense (which I doubt), he will listen to me and the billions of Raj-o-philes around the world.

Yours angrily,

Raj

P.S. The piece of fudge I crushed in my bare hand is available to buy in my shop at half price.

Sign Raj's petition here:

www.worldofwalliams.com/bringbackraj

DISCOVER

www.worldofwalliams.com

Visit Raj's shop and...

*play super-silly games

*collect points for Raj's whoopee surprise

*join the Wallichums and top
the leaderboard

*enter amazing competitions to
win incredible prizes

And much much more!